TENDERFOOT

An American Mammoths Novel

Airship 27 Productions

Published by Airship 27 Productions
www.airship27.com
www.airship27hangar.com

Editor: Ron Fortier
Associate Editor: Fred Adams Jr.
Marketing and Promotions Manager: Michael Vance
Production Designer: Rob Davis

ISBN: 978-1-969285-08-0

Produced in the United States of America

10 9 8 7 6 5 4 3 2 1

TENDERFOOT

An American Mammoths Novel

By Michael Panush

CHAPTER ONE

A Congregation of Alligators

A gentle touch tickled my cheek, wedged as it was in the flagstones of some dingy alley. Light, ticklish, and wonderfully cool. It might belong to some gentle lover. But it didn't. My eyes flickered open, my headache doubling in pain as gray sunlight flashed in from the top of the alley. The touch belonged to a trunk which belonged to a mammoth. A Columbian mammoth.

My mammoth.

"Will you stop your damn tickling!" I attempted a command, but the rasp in my throat transformed my words into a slurred murmur—akin to the squelching of a heavy footfall driving into Missouri mud. I sat up, the world spinning around me. Stained walls, an overcast sky threatening rain, and a puddle of olive-colored vomit that may have spewed from my very mouth. Another beautiful section of Bourbon Street, in the Free City of New Orleans.

And there, seated on his haunches at the edge of the alley, like a tremendous hound, was my mammoth. General Butler, the so-called "Beast" who had once conquered this city. My beast had a sloping head, a pair of massive tusks that ground against the walls of the alley, and thick legs with wrinkled knees. His tan fur, thin and scruffy, waved slightly and in the wind, and his dark eyes shone—a pair of black jewels in his friendly, wizened face.

Somehow, I made it to my feet. General Butler's trunk went around my shoulder—a friendly boa constrictor. I pushed it aside. "Confounded animal. I was soundly asleep."

A disconsolate trumpeting was my response.

I'd been with Butler long enough to know that meant he was hungry.

"Very well, very well. You want breakfast? We'll get some breakfast." I brushed rainwater—at least, I hoped it was rainwater—from my shearling vest and found my Stetson lying on the cobblestones. A quick smoothing back of my hair and beard and I was entirely presentable.

We decamped for the city. My stomach and head suffered in miserable tandem. I didn't much desire breakfast, but some solid rations were probably necessary to end the bloody campaign raging in my skull, spine, and belly. And a stiff drink also wouldn't go amiss.

Hair of the Dog.

General Butler and I emerged from the alley and onto Bourbon Street itself. Those fine buildings, a riot of color, with their verandas and wrought-iron balconies stretching above. It swelled with horse and camel-pulled coaches, stately travelers enjoying the promenade, fiddlers and banjo-strummers on the corner plucking out tunes for pennies. The General followed behind me, his trunk swaying. Heavy feet settling against paving stones.

What time was it? I had slipped into oblivion when it was dark, and now the sun was a greasy speck at the center of the sky.

Forget breakfast. This would be lunch.

Butler and I went around the corner to a gambling establishment, one of many in the Free City. This one was called the Jolly Sloth and the sign featured a ground sloth in a jester's bell-draped hat grinning sardonically at his hand of cards. It was a decent establishment. I'd known that, for I remembered entering the night before, and no feeling of dismay lingered. Then again, I'd drunken myself into oblivion. Details were scant.

I had Butler stand by the hitching post outside. A good mammoth, and far smarter than any horse. He would not stray. Not unless something tasty or interesting went by.

I shoved open the door. A concierge or steward or guard—or some combination of the three—glowered at me. He wore a white evening jacket with a red rose in the lapel and his hairless head shone like the fang of a saber-toothed tiger. He sneered at me. "Corporal Clement Clarke. You're back, eh?"

"That I am."

"Hallelujah." He looked past me at Butler. "You'll be wanting your animal fed, I expect."

"General Butler, my friend, deserves nothing but the finest leavings from your kitchen." I fixed this steward with a steely glare. "He's a hero, goddamn it. Rode with the 2nd Elephantine Dragoons throughout the entire war, from the Siege of Vicksburg to the March to the Sea. All the way to Appomattox."

"Did he now?"

This bald-headed bastard most likely fought for the other side. "Send someone to your kitchen. Bring out a barrel of water, and another of wine—any vintage will do, the General is not picky—and a crate of vegetables." Now, the final part of my argument. "Otherwise, I shall spend my money at another establishment. A much kinder one than this godforsaken dump."

He sighed. "Arguing with you is more trouble than its worth. At least you're sober this time." He stood aside. "Go in and find yourself a seat at the table. I'll see to your elephant."

Elephants—folks used that word in place of mammoths now and then. Like buffalo for bison. "He's a Mammoth. Columbian Mammoth. The King of the Plains." I spun around and waved to Butler. "Be good, General."

He trumpeted happily.

Then I entered the Jolly Sloth and found my way straight to the gaming table.

It wasn't a godforsaken dump. In fact, the Jolly Sloth was the sort of high-class joint that gave you every comfort as it fleeced you. Chairs and tables, all in red velvet, and polished brass on the roulette wheels. Dealers in crimson vests expertly worked the decks, and gamblers fanned the cards in their white gloves. I settled at the nearest poker table, asked to be dealt in, and sought about filling my stomach.

A pair of prairie oysters, to help settle my belly, and a plate of beignets fairly drowned in powdered sugar to fill it. A wonderous way to start a man's day.

Then, I accepted my cards and began to play.

Poker—one of the greatest past-times ever crafted by the sages of old. I played with aplomb, swelling my pot, losing occasionally, but always upping my stake. Most of the players were mere amateurs. An officer from Gran-Haiti, with his epaulets and braid. Some visiting Yankee businessman in his broadcloth suit and graying Van Dyke. But one fellow, the dandy son of some local shipping magnate by the name of Xavier St. James, clearly knew his way around a deck of cards. He had burnished blonde hair a moustache fused into place with tonic, a Panama hat to go with this white suit, and a cane with a topper that had to be mammoth ivory. For the ivory in that cane, I despised him.

The fact that my luck vanished and he cleaned me out with alarming rapidity did nothing to endear myself to his few charms.

"And so, Corporal Clarke, the tide appears to have turned." He grinned to himself as he reached out an arm and encircled the pot, dragging it all to his side of the table. "Rotten luck, my friend. Rotten luck indeed. But I am a generous fellow, am I not? I'll give you a chance to win it back."

"You're a horse's ass," I replied.

He arched an eyebrow—blonde, so it was nearly invisible. "Vulgarity. Is that to be your refuge? Or will you defend your honor on the field, so to speak?"

The cards came for the next hand, the dealer wetting his lips. Perhaps expecting trouble. I gazed at my hand. A decent draw—a King and a Jack that might turn into something more, given a little assistance.

St. James tittered and made his bet, one that I could not hope to match. He looked at the little pile of chips as the others saw his bet. "I seem to have you at a disadvantage, corporal. You shall have to retreat from the table—something I believe a military gentleman such as yourself would be loath to do. Thankfully, a solution occurs to me."

The prairie oyster in my gut felt like it had turned to lead. "What'd that be?"

He nodded toward the window, currently overlooking General Butler's backside. "That beast out there. The Columbian. He is yours?"

Right now, Butler's trunk had snaked out and grabbed the straw hat from a passing lady. He popped it into his mouth like a piece of kettle corn.

"That's right."

"I shall take him instead of money." He fixed me with a cool gaze. "No man is poor if he owns a mammoth. The creature is a cornucopia of profit. The ivory of the tusks is worth a considerable fortune, and the same with the fur."

Now, my headache returned—but burning hot this time. I stood, glaring at Xavier St. James. "You ought to stop talking."

"Then there's the meat. The heart alone can create a sizeable feast and my family's chef would delight at all the possibilities..."

I drew my howdah pistol, a double-barreled monster that I'd carried since boyhood for stopping predators in the Kansas Plains, from its place on my hip.

St. James had about a moment to scream before I shoved the barrel of the howdah pistol into his face. His wide mouth was just big enough to accommodate the gun's muzzle. He tilted back on his chair, arms flailing, and I grabbed the lapel of his seersucker to stop him from falling.

"Say another word and I'll put your brains on the goddamn tile!"

Of course, he couldn't say another word even if he wanted to. His mouth was too full of gun.

He stared at me with pleading eyes as the other gamblers scrambled away and the dealer raised both hands pleadingly.

"Corporal. Ahem." I looked up. The bouncer stood there, his coat open to reveal a revolver. "I think you had better call it quits."

And he was right. What good would it do, getting into a gunfight in a gambling hall? Or bullying some no-account dandy for insulting my mammoth? I was already broke. Having to spend the night in jail, or worse, wouldn't improve my situation. I still had Butler to consider after all.

I withdrew my howdah pistol, holstered it, and picked up my remaining chip. That I sent to the dealer as a tip—it amounted for little, though it did salvage my pride—and I strutted calmly to the door. A slick little puddle grew under Xavier St. James. There was justice yet in this wretched world.

It wouldn't be too bad. I had two nickels to rub together, after all, and the means to earn more.

The bounty hunter's trade. It wasn't for everyone—that was certainly the case. But as long as I had bullets in my gun-belt and General Butler stomping along beneath me, I could find some owlhoot who'd run afoul of the law and bring them in for the bounty. Elephant rustlers, bank robbers, road agents, and ne'er-do-wells of all stripes could be transformed into enough folding money to put myself into the comfortable embrace of another drunk after a night of joy at the card-house.

That was how I had made my living, ever since abandoning the Elephantry in the years after the war. Getting shot at for soldier's wages seemed a poor substitute for going into business myself. Bounty hunting had its ups and downs, of course—an awful lot of downs lately—but I could track, hunt, intimidate, and shoot with the best of them. And General Butler certainly made up for any of my shortcomings.

I just had to find a suitable Wanted poster.

I stumbled back outside, into the sunlight. The steward slammed the door behind me, and the noise and the harsh glare made my headache do its little dance all over again. My boots settled on the sidewalk. Where was that noticeboard and the posters?

"Sir?" A girl appeared in front of me. "Sir, are you Corporal Clement Clarke? Of the 2nd Elephantine Dragoons?"

I regarded this newcomer, who seemed to have emerged complete from the mist. She was about eleven years of age, with hair the color of freshly-ploughed dirt, and bright eyes. Something Celestial about her as well, though her dress was white and lacey, with a high collar, and she wore a straw boater's hat and tall riding boots. At one of her boots, a tiny horse—a dawn horse, about the size of a cocker-spaniel—stared up at me. Its mane had been braided and it wore a fancy red velvet ribbon.

A dozen responses came to mind at her sudden arrival, her little companion, and her line of questioning. Only one emerged. "You've got a real tiny horse there, missy."

She rested her hand on the horse's head. "Her name is Lady."

Lady let out a little whicker at General Butler, who responded with a trumpet.

"And my name is Thalia. Thalia Ridgeway." She cleared her throat. "My father is Rufus Ridgeway."

A shudder crept under my skin. Rufus. I remembered him. He rode alongside me in the war—always ready with a joke when the going got grim. Which it often did. I'd left the Elephantine Dragoons, and he had stayed on.

"How is Rufus, then?"

"Dead, sir." She grimaced. "And I need your help."

I considered it—for half-a-second. "Can you pay me?"

Hesitance. She opened her mouth and then shut it. Well, that was answer enough.

Maybe that was for the best. What could I do anyhow?

I let out a long sigh and turned away. "I'm not interested, Miss Ridgeway. Your father was a good man. You got my condolences. And my apologies." I started up the sidewalk, bound for the noticeboard.

"Corporal Clarke!" She sprang after me, a pale tornado accompanied by her tiny horse. "I beg of you, sir—hear me out. I face great danger. Grave peril. And so does the country. I must task you with a solemn and terrible mission. Once you hear about it, you won't turn away from the task." I was liking the sound of this less and less. "Please, sir—I've fled from the home of my grandparents in St. Louis. I have risked everything—including my father's assassins—to come and find you. I need your help, sir. Dearly."

By then, I had reached the noticeboard. I examined the mass of advertisements for cure-all-tonics, cheetah races, and political advertisements focused on everything from the Masonic menace to the Fenian Cause. One caught my eye. I snatched it free from the board and held it up to the misty sunlight.

"Corporal Clarke." The Ridgeway Girl had reached me. She planted her feet and glared up at me. "Corporal Clarke, are you listening to me?"

"Virginia Wells, alias One-Eyed Ginny." I read from the Wanted Poster, above an inky sketch of One-Eyed Ginny herself—her short hair framing a face flecked with knife scars rendered like shadows in the ink. Reading it loud to drown out Thalia Ridgeway's caterwauling. "Wanted for bank robbery, train robbery, and murder." Oh, Ginny, you been keeping yourself busy.

I ran my fingers along the reward money. All those happy little zeros, lined up in a row. I stuffed the Wanted poster in my pocket. "Sorry, Miss Ridgeway. I'm busy."

"Busy?" She sputtered. "You're a bounty hunter. Fair enough. That's your trade—even if it is a lowly one for a former Federal Dragoon such as yourself." A blast of girlish disdain in her words. "And I don't have much money to pay you." Her manner brightened. "But this is more important than a bounty. More important than a thousand bounties."

"It is, huh?"

She bobbed her head, her eyes huge.

"Then it's all the more important that you find someone else to be your champion." I walked around to General Butler's side, where a little rope-ladder dangled down from his howdah. "You can see for yourself that I ain't suitable for much more than two or three bounties, much less a thousand." I clutched the ladder and scrambled up.

Thalia remained on the sidewalk. "There may be some others. Former comrades-in-arms of my father's. But you're the closest."

"I'm working on running away. You'd better let me."

I pulled myself into the howdah. A stretch of old quilt, with assorted saddle-bags and panniers strewn about. I searched them. Old bullets, crumpled papers, a squirrel pelt—how long had it been since I cleaned these things? Finally,

I found what I was looking for: a bottle of rotgut, half-full of amber joy. I clutched that as I shimmied up to General Butler's neck and wedged my legs behind his ears.

The mahout's seat.

She stared up, small now from the seat, and picked up her little dawn horse like it was a child's stuffed doll. "Please, Corporal." Her face had gone pale. Was she trying not to cry? "You fought for a good cause once before. Please—will not you do so again?

I rested a hand on General Butler's bumpy head. With the other, I took the final slug of whiskey. "Goodbye, Miss Ridgeway. I can offer you a wish of good luck. But nothing more."

Then I gave the bottle a toss, letting it fall and shatter in the gutter. Not enough to hit her, but the crash made her jump back with a squeak. She recovered quickly, starting into another plea.

But I had already swayed my knees and whistled and Butler began his plodding, undaunted trot down the street. We left Thalia Ridgeway fuming on the sidewalk. We had places to be, after all. And a bounty to catch.

By that afternoon, we'd arrived at the swamp. The bayou, to use the proper name. It stretched all around, composed of endless thickets of watery wood, split with countless sprays of cypress and the drapery of Spanish moss. Muddy waterways cut across the sloping islands and bluffs, ranging from little creeks and fat ponds to full-on rivers winding their way through the trees. The place hummed with life. Birds conversed endlessly, raccoons rustled, and an occasional wildcat scream or swamp sloth cry blazed like the Rebel Yell through the underbrush.

Plenty of insects too. They buzzed around me mercilessly, no matter how many I slapped. General Butler kept his tail whirring, and that saved his hindquarters, but they'd make their bites anyway. I had some unguent that I'd picked up in Yazoo City which would help ease his itching, later on.

How the wild mammoths—and there were a few left who made the swamp their home—dealt with it, I didn't know.

Butler mastered the terrain. He could shove aside any brush, wade through the gullies, and swim like he was born to the water. Thanks to him, I made good time. Heading for the place where we'd find One-Eyed Ginny.

The General had made such fine progress when we were fighting the Vicksburg Campaign. It was river fighting then, and the pounding feet of infantry, the wheels of cannon, and even the galloping hooves of horses failed at navigating that Tennessee and Mississippi bottomland—but the mammoths could do it, and Ulysses S. Grant kept us right busy. It was pulling barges, clearing brush, towing the heavy artillery pieces, and scouting ahead, all under the guns of Johnny Reb.

And we fought. We got our fill of it, and still there was more fighting to be done.

The Battle of the Blood River Ridge—all of it was bad but I think Blood River Ridge was the worst. The Confederates had a bit of high ground overlooking a mass of swampy, watery river country, and they could pour down rifle and cannon fire on the advancing Union troops without a care in the world. General Grant gave the order—the Elephantry would advance down the middle, followed by the infantry, while the cavalry worked the flank. We even had something to put the odds in our favor—little cannons, falconets, set in our howdahs, complete with two-man crews to work them.

Didn't exactly go as planned.

My loader lasted about a minute before some Rebel sharpshooter caught him straight in the skull. He fell back, his brains sloshing down and running sticky into my mammoth's fur. But there was no stopping now. I bent low, tightening my knees, and urged Butler right up the hill. Panting, just like him.

Those blasts were raining down amongst us, casting up earth and water, rifle bullets whining like lunatic mosquitoes, and the ridgeline seemed no closer. Mammoths were strong all right, but they were big targets, and many dropped—but we kept going, our little guns firing back all the while and putting white, choking puff-clouds every which way. The thunder of guns, trumpeting mammoths, screeches and wails of dying men and animals, and so much blood that the iron tang of it choked me. God, that was hell.

Then the rebels decided to unleash their own elephants. To try and charge and bring us down. Their mammoths came rushing in, screeching, and flailing their trunks, tusks shining as their riders fired away with rifle and revolver. Not the smartest decision. But I guess them Southern gentlemen who put bows in their mammoth fur and fed them the finest corn wanted to be chivalrous knights or something. And chivalrous knights need to charge.

One came barreling straight for me, a beautiful creature with combed blonde fur and a caparison in Confederate colors with 'Lincoln-Killer' inscribed on the side. Charged down right after our little cannon had fired its last shell and Butler's foot had gotten stuck in a mudhole.

Yes, sir. I thought I was finished. The knowledge of my doom creeping up so sudden that I didn't have time to be afraid. But then the rebel elephant was bashed aside, and its driver blasted dead from a scatter-gun wielded by none other than Rufus Ridgeway.

Even as his mount, a Wooly named Constance, caught a chunk of grapeshot to the belly that ended her life.

The Battle of Blood River Ridge finished soon after. The cavalry came right around the flanks, and fixed the Rebels in place—and then the elephants and the men made it up and finished them. A hard-won victory. That was General Grant's way—pounding away at the enemy ranks, not giving them respite nor a chance to retreat, and he forged it all in the swampy mess of the Vicksburg Campaign.

And afterwards, he joined me and Rufus by the body of Constance, watching as my friend had his arms around her head, her trunk weakly embracing him, and her chest rose and fell with pained and labored breaths. Grant removed his cap and his eyes shone with sadness as I gave Rufus my howdah pistol and he placed it to the skull of Constance and ended her suffering for good.

We'd all suffered, but we had each other and we had our flag.

And now Rufus was gone, I didn't know what had happened to the nation, and I'd wandered away from a child who needed a helping hand. Chasing down some no-account bounty instead.

General Butler's trunk snaked up and gave my cheek a pat. I perked up. He'd smelled something.

"Easy there." I stiffened my knees a little and he slowed.

Up ahead, the big branch of a tree jutted out over the water. A man sat on it. A big crow on a fence. He had faded jeans, a long black duster, and a crumbling stovepipe hat. A lean leathery face, lips screwed up around a long-stemmed pipe fashioned from a monkey skull. Looked like an undertaker who hadn't been paid in a while.

Except for the Sharps rifle on his back and the pair of fancy pistols on his hip.

"Howdy." Burning prairie grass in his voice.

"Howdy to you," I replied. "Orrin Prong."

We'd known each other. Similar trades. Except, while I brought in outlaws, Prong killed just about anyone if the price was right. He stood on the branch, perching lightly, and leaned against the tree trunk.

A little sweat thickened on my spine. Was he here for me? If he was, why wasn't I dead already? Then again, Prong had odd habits. They say he liked to look his kills in the eye, to watch the life leave them.

Butler let out a deep grunt and stomped a foot, spraying muck.

"Your elephant don't like me much," Prong said.

I leaned back in my seat. "He don't like many people."

"Guess we're similar." He spewed smoke from his nostrils. "In that regard."

"What are you doing here, Prong?"

"I'm gonna pose that question to you, friend." Those eyes belonged on a wolf, one that was just about to take a bite into your arm. "What are you doing in this swamp?"

I looked into those cold eyes and knew I couldn't lie to him—he'd see right through it. "Searching out One-Eyed Ginny. Figure she'd hole up at the Renault Place. Was planning to go there and ask for her." If he wanted Ginny, I might just let him have her. There was no way to dissuade Prong short of killing him. I might have General Butler on my side, but Prong was a titan in the field of slaughter. That was a fight I'd lose—even if I wanted to have it. "Now what about you?"

He shrugged. "One-Eyed Ginny Wells, huh? Go on and get her, then. I'm not interested."

Then he settled back on the branch and drew out a silver harmonica from his pocket. He placed it to his lips and started playing. He wasn't particularly good at it. Made a sort of noxious hum, rising and falling like breath.

General Butler snorted and shook his tusks, agitated by the noise, and I tightened my heels and sent him tromping along, further into the swamp.

Relief crept on me. Prong was minding his own business and I'd go ahead and let him.

It was around the evening when I came to the Renault Place. They had transformed a trio of islands surrounded by thick natural moats into a little fortress, with a set of outposts on sticks rising from the muck. Bridges connected their houses and an extended beach offered a place where they could set their pirogues to the water and turn a barbecued beast on a spit. Right now, they were doing just that—holding a little shindig complete with fancy fiddling, fresh-baked cornbread, and carving up a glyptodont—one of them giant armadillos—that they'd roasted in its shell.

No sentries to worry about. And why would there be? The Renaults were the king swamp rats of the bayou. Made their living offering sanctuary to criminals who had been thrown out of every other bandit den and outlaw roost. One-Eyed Ginny Wells had no doubt been accepted into their fold. For a hefty fee, of course.

They banqueted with their guns. Every swamp rat there was armed and there was no way I could manage all of them, even with Butler backing my play. I thought for a moment. A daring plan—many would call it foolhardy and many more would call it stupid—came to mind.

I directed Butler closer. Hard to hide a mammoth, even in dense underbrush, so I moved quick. First, I slid my buffalo rifle out of its scabbard and loaded it up. Then, I got General Butler in the right position—and I whistled to make him charge.

He crossed the moat, snorting and trumpeting and waving his trunk about so the moonlight caught the huge sweep of his tusks. The water went up to his knees, and then the joints of his legs, and finally pressed against his furry flanks and soaked my legs—and still he kept coming.

The Renaults paused in their merry-making. The fiddler continued, picking out a few happy notes before trailing off and going silent. I had General Butler charge right up to the beach and smash aside a stack of pirogues with his tusks. They shattered, the flimsy boats spilling down, breaking apart, and bouncing their way across the beach. That showed we meant business.

They started going for their guns, but I already had the rifle out and aimed—right at Mama Renault. "You even think about it and I'll put a round right in her, I swear to God!"

A second of silence. Mama Renault's kin looked at their mother. About a score of them—all hard-bitten swamp rats. They wore rumpled checkered shirts, big boots, and kept their sideburns thick and their beards long. They looked like they wrestled gators every day of the week and beat up swamp sloths on Sundays. But I had the buffalo rifle, and that meant I held the cards.

Their eyes went to their matriarch. Old Mama Renault, seated in a rocking chair on the porch. "Do what he says, boys. Lower your irons."

"But Mama..." One giant swamp rat asked.

"Do what I say or I'll send you into the swamp to get a switch. Tan your hide until you holler." Mama Renault seemed oddly unconcerned about a rifle aimed in her direction. She worked a mass of chewing tobacco in her cheek—worked it furiously. Her sons did as they were told, carefully setting down every gun.

But I was sitting on a powder keg and lighting a dozen matches.

"Hey there, Mama Renault," I said, trying to sound polite.

"Clement Clarke." She had a pure Cajun drawl. "Who are you looking for, Corporal—you goddamn Yankee?"

"I'm from Kansas, ma'am."

"That's Yankee to me. Now answer my goddamn question."

"Virginia Wells, ma'am. One-Eyed Ginny."

She squinted and chewed a little more. This time, the chewing tobacco leaked out from her mouth and spilled down her chin in a creeping orange tide. Stains on her bib overalls told me that it had leaked many times before. But Mama Renault could still cause me and Butler plenty of trouble, if she had a mind to.

"What if I told you One-Eyed Ginny ain't here?" she asked.

"I wouldn't believe you, ma'am. Ginny's on the run, and this is the best place for outlaws to hide out." I kept the rifle raised, casually aimed in her house's direction. "I don't got money to pay you. But I can make plenty of trouble, especially with this beast under me. And One-Eyed Ginny already paid. If I take her away, you can keep that money."

Mama Renault considered it and chewed some more. "I think you're the one in for some trouble, Corporal Mammoth. More than you bargained for. See, we don't get much entertainment out here in the swamp. You just provided us with some."

Quick as lighting, that old woman reached over. A lever projected up from the porch and she slammed it down. I couldn't do a damn thing about it. I could shoot her, I suppose—but her boys would cut me down a moment later. She knew it, and gave me a witch's grin as the lever went all the way down.

Gears went to work somewhere in their ramshackle estate and a wooden gate rolled itself open, revealing a deep pool of black water.

"Your animal's big, all right. But that don't make him God on the throne. Not in this swamp."

Something split the water. A bit of whiteness. The outline moved under the surface, heading purposefully out and into the moat.

"Guess what, Corporal Mammoth? You're about to meet the Tarasque!"

The water went frothy and the biggest alligator—a snow white gator—I'd ever seen burst out of the water. This was the Tarasque, no doubt, some legendary monster akin to the leviathan or the dragon that St. George butchered all those years ago. Butler made a panicked huffing noise and stepped back, his heavy feet splashing as the gator's jaws snapped shut inches from his trunk. He backed up quick, eyes darting about and trunk held high.

Then the gator vanished.

Laughter from Renault's boys. "Don't shoot them now! Don't shoot either of them!" Mama Renault's voice carried over the merriment. "This fight is between beasts alone. Afterwards—when we're cooking up whatever mammoth the Tarasque don't want, we'll settle with Clarke." Did that rule apply to me? Then again, if I took a shot at the gator, the swamp rats would cut me down before I could reload.

So I guess it was a contest of beasts after all.

The Tarasque was smaller than General Butler, no doubt about it. But his jaws could still work a number of Butler's legs, and my mammoth couldn't do much about it. Or he could swim right under, get a bite on Butler's belly or even his throat, and open him up with those big nasty jaws of his. I hated to think of it. The water was the Tarasque's homeland and Butler was the stranger. The edge went to the reptile.

I kept my calm. Hard to do, given Butler's shuffling steps and the pale monster in the water below us.

Then a splash and the Tarasque burst out yet again. This time from the side. Its jaws flashed, opening wide as the horizon. Going for a bite into Butler's flank. Water splashed, those teeth clenched home, and Butler made a panicked grunt in pain as red flowed. He shook and twisted, landing a hit on the gator with his tusks, and that alone saved him. The Tarasque went back into the swamp water.

Preparing to strike again.

Blood dripped from the wound. Shallow—but it had to hurt. I patted Butler's skull, trying to make soothing noises. God, it hurt to see my best friend take such a blow. Especially when there wasn't a damn thing I could do about it.

Hoots and laughs from the shore. "Tarrasque's got a big belly, Clarke!" Mama Renault cried. "Room for both of you in them pearly scales!"

Butler trumpeted and stomped—wanting to break free. To fight his way. I swallowed and relaxed my grip. Okay, General—let's see what you can do.

He dashed back, stepping carefully through the water. Waving tusks and trunk to disturb it with ripples as he walked back—going for the muddy bank behind us. A retreat? What was he doing?

Then he came up, emerging from the water. Returning to dry land. Muddy water dripped from his fur as he stood his ground and waited.

The Tarasque emerged again—bursting from the water and scrambling up. Going on land.

Where Butler had the edge.

First, the General's foot lashed out. A good kick, driving against the Tarasque's snout. Hisses and thrashing from the gator, but he couldn't dive under the water now. General Butler trumpeted in triumph and struck.

His trunk lashed around the Tarasque's neck and he hauled it up, its big tail flailing. For half-a-second, the gator was hoisted clear in the air. Then General Butler sent him flying with a flick of his trunk—transforming him into a white, scaly projectile.

My mammoth—he was a keen strategist. I shouldn't have doubted him.

The Tarasque crashed into the beach, upsetting the roasting giant armadillo. It hissed, snapped its jaws, and scrambled away, sending the Renaults scattering. Its muzzle pierced the water and it slipped in again.

Then paddled away. Probably looking to tangle with smaller prey.

Silence on the swamp. Renault's boys looked in misery at their fleeing champion.

Now, I let the buffalo rifle roar. It boomed away, blasting apart the porch

…he hauled it up, it's big tail flailing…

next to her. Splinters flew as the echo hit the swamp. Quick as could be, I snatched another bullet and slid it into position. "Mama Renault, I am tired and it is growing late. Fetch One-Eyed Ginny, will you? I'd like to be on my way."

She let out another mass of spit—a stream that squirted expertly into the dirt. Then she nodded to two of her sons, burly gents trying to salvage the roasting glyptodont. Wordlessly, they went inside. I will say this for the Renaults: they knew when they were beat. They vanished inside the central cabin.

Harsh noises from inside. Shouts, snarls, curses—and then the door slammed open and One-Eyed Ginny sprinted outside, trying to make her escape. Mama Renault's boys tackled her and hauled her back, even as she fought, snarled, and spat. She was scrawny and rangy, clad in a rumpled shirt, old trousers, and a fringed jacket, her hair cut brutally short and an alligator-skin eye-patch hiding one eye.

She reminded me of one of them hunting monster birds from down south. I'd seen one in a zoo in Dallas once, all shiny feathers and nasty beak. One-Eyed Ginny was maybe more dangerous, though.

They shoved her in front of Butler. I reached back, unrolled the rope ladder, and aimed the rifle at her. "Good to see you, Ginny."

"Burn in Hell, bounty hunter!" She rose to her knees, spitting out hate and maybe considering making a run for it. "You and your stinking elephant!"

"Same wonderful attitude." I whistled and Butler stomped closer. "Get on up or I'll put one in your leg."

She relented, cursing me still as she clambered up. Made it up to the howdah. "Dammit, I bet you got lice in this old quilt. When was the last time you got it washed?" I crept back, crawling a little closer, and drew out a set of manacles that I'd picked up from a US Marshal in Tupelo. "Course, I could say the same about you, Corporal Clarke. You smell like you fell out of your mammoth's behind. That and a distillery."

"Uh-huh." I snapped the manacles on and tucked the key into my pocket—then worked a cord around her ankles. Just in case. "That feel all right?"

"You know it don't."

"Good. Just sit down. We'll get you to the Free City soon enough. Gotta decide where you're going—Gran-Haiti or the Federal government. Depends on who's paying the most." I shuffled back to the Butler's neck. "Don't try nothing now. I can spin round and put one through you before the thought crosses your mind." Then I faced Mama Renault and touched my finger to the brim of my hat. "Obliged to you, ma'am."

"You're a *loup garou*, Clarke." Mama Renault glared right back. "Part of you is beast and part of you is man. You need to decide which is which." Then she faced her boys. "So much for the Tarasque. We need a pet that will stand up against a mammoth. I'm through with gators. Get me one of them goddamn giant snakes!"

I turned Butler around and started back. Part beast and part man. Right now, all of me was tired and eager to get paid.

Darkness came quick and I started looking around for a place to make camp. Spending a night with One-Eyed Ginny Wells for company wasn't an appealing prospect, but it beat trampling around in the dark with her behind me. I had a lantern in one of the saddlebags and a little pole that hooked onto General Butler's bridle. It cast a shallow beam of light up ahead, glistening on dark waters and stretches of mud. The cottonmouths would be slithering in those waters soon enough.

Wells didn't sound tired. She kept on complaining, even as I tried to find a decent island for our camp. "Holy God, Clarke—you're a scarecrow which some country jokers have equipped with a holster and a revolver. Except that you smell worse than any scarecrow I've ever seen. I've been hunted by lawmen of all sorts, and when it comes to being a sorry sack of dung, you've got them all beat."

"Well, you're the one I caught, Ginny Wells. So what does that say about you?"

"How about you untie me, slick, and we'll see how good you are?"

Butler grunted, his trunk arching—a furry cobra. I raised a hand. "Quit your yapping."

He had smelled something. I had him plod onto a soggy island topped with a grove, and looked around. Something rustled in the brush. A panther? A sloth? Prong?

"Who's out there?" I demanded.

The branches parted and a mule emerged. Young Thalia Ridgeway rode in the saddle, her little horse Lady tucked into a saddlebag. The mule had mud all over its legs and looked about ready to collapse into the swamp, and Thalia didn't look much better. She tugged at the reins and the mule came to a halt. At least she rode well—her bearing telling me that she was no stranger to the saddle.

Wells poked her head over my shoulder. "It's a little Celestial girl."

"I'm nearly twelve," Thalia replied. "Not so little, I would say."

"You are little," I repeated. "And foolish. Damn foolish—wandering around in a swamp, alone, at this hour. I can't count the number of ways you could meet your end. How'd you even find me?"

"Your mammoth, sir." A weak smile. "Big footprints."

"Well, ain't you clever, then?" Anger rose up, hot and thick and spilling into my words. "Goddamn, you're Rufus's only child and you're gonna throw your life away..."

"I needed to find you, corporal," she replied. "I judged it worth the risk."

"What do you want with a sorry heap of mammoth chips like him?" Wells asked.

"I need him, ma'am. The country needs him. But for the moment, I fear I am being followed and I need protection. An assassin—clad in black. He wears a stovepipe hat."

Prong. So that's who he was after.

I swallowed. The worry came thick now—fear for Thalia.

Tried to play it off—to be callous. "Well, you've found me. We might as well stop here for the night and make camp." Too dangerous to keep going. I urged General Butler further, up onto the island. "We'll get a fire going. Then, next morning, I'm taking Miss Wells here to the law." I gave her a nudge with my shoulder, sending her falling into the howdah. "And you are going straight back to St. Louis, to your grandparents." Did Prong hunt at night? I'd have to take the chance.

She said nothing. I hadn't outwitted her—she was merely tired.

I descended from Butler, tugged Wells off so that she plopped in the mud, and had her sit on one of my old bedrolls while Thalia and I made camp and I tended to Butler's bites. The girl handled herself well enough, for one used to the cities, as we got some kindling for a fire and hobbled her mule.

"My father," she explained, as I pulled down a bedroll for her—I'd use an old buffalo robe for mine. "He'd often take me camping. But nothing like this. We'd have a full tent, a servant with a donkey bringing supplies, and cook ribeye steak right over the fire."

Wells sat up. "I reckon Corporal Clarke don't got ribeye steak."

"You reckon right." I drew our vittles from the saddle bags. Some old cuts of beef jerky and hardtack. We'd have that for breakfast as well. Butler got to eat better—he used his trunk to grab vegetation and pop it into his mouth, chewing continuously.

Then Thalia surprised me. "I got something for him, actually." She went to the mule and took out a package of oats for her tiny horse—and a mango for Butler. His trunk snaked out, snatched it away, and he popped it in his mouth—then let out a delighted grunt. She smiled with girlish delight.

I couldn't help grinning at his joy. "Your father always took good care of his mammoths."

She perked up. "He had an Alaskan Woolly, right?"

"Constance by name." Clearly, she wanted a story. A suitable one came to mind. "She got sick once—trouble with the rations, maybe—and she got the runs something awful. But he stood by her, combing her hair, bringing her fresh vegetables that we'd foraged. Even though he got fairly bathed in runny mammoth crap." Well, maybe that wasn't the most suitable.

But Thalia listened. "That does sound like him."

"A big heart," I agreed.

That made Wells let out a braying harpy laugh. "Unlike you, Corporal Clarke. You got no heart at all."

I didn't respond. Thalia fell silent as well, the quiver of her lips showing her worry.

We went silent, staring into the fire as it burned a little lower. I crunched on the jerky, chewing mightily to make it fit for swallowing. The others did too. General Butler settled down on his belly to sleep and I leaned back, resting against his vast, furry side. For the past several years, this had been my life. Wake up in some measure of drunkenness, ride out in search of an outlaw, haul them back to town for the money, spend it on whiskey and cards, and then repeat the whole process over and over again.

Now, here was Thalia Ridgeway, a kid as unused to the wilderness as the little horse she called Lady—asking for my help. After her father had saved my life. All I could do was turn her down and keep singing the same song again.

"I'll get you home safe to St. Louis," I told her. "Your grandparents—they'll deal with the situation."

"They despise me. Keep me away from other children, confined to our estate. Tutors come in and see to my schooling. They'll probably shuffle me off to some foreign mission as soon as I'm of age and delight in my absence."

Wells shook her head. "That's a damn shame. How could anyone hate you, darling?"

She hesitated.

"It's all right. You can tell us."

"Well, there's the matter of my parentage." She looked away. "Celestial, you know. My mother—she was Chinese. Worked on our railroad concern. All I have are stories. My grandparents arranged for her departure soon after I was born. Trying to hush up a scandal."

And these were the people to whom I'd bring Thalia back. It hurt to consider it. The world couldn't be an easy place for someone like Thalia and I wasn't doing a damn thing to make it any easier.

"Well, what else am I to do?" I asked the fire. "What do I know about raising a child?"

"I can handle myself, sir. I'm old enough. And we have more to do than worry about my rearing. Much more."

"There's your talk of grand conspiracy and national peril. I don't care about it. Country's already gone straight to Hell. How much worse can it get?"

General Butler suddenly gave out a little snort, rising up and making my head nearly plop in the mud. He had detected something.

A shout came from the clearing. "Corporal Clarke?" That voice—raised in volume, but not in passion. Still bone-dry. It was Prong.

He was somewhere in the darkness. Goddamn it—he did hunt by night after all.

I sprang up, drawing the revolver from my belt and gripping the howdah pistol. Where the hell was he?

"I got a bead on you, Clarke."

"Is that so?" I stood, looking out into the darkness. Lots of shadows, fronds and leafy branches waving in the wind. Like fighting a ghost. "I thought you said you weren't interested in One-Eyed Ginny?" I moved in front of Thalia. Her back was to a stout oak—that blocked any shot at the girl, who held Lady close and shuddered.

"I don't want you or her. Why I ain't shot you yet. Call it professional courtesy. I want the girl."

"Pretty lowdown, killing a girl ain't even a woman yet."

"It's her pa's fault. If he hadn't talked to her before I paid him a visit, we wouldn't be having this problem. Now step aside. My professional courtesy don't go that far."

"Clarke!" It was Ginny. She had rolled over and crawled a little closer to the fire. "Uncuff me! Give me a pistol—I can shoot the legs off a flea. You know it's true! Two of us together, we got a chance against Prong."

"Shut up!" I glowered at her. We had another chance. I patted General Butler's flank. Next to me, the fire burned bright. "You and me draw iron, Prong, and it could go badly for you!" I raised my voice, shouting into the darkness. But you might as well bargain with a dire wolf. I snapped my fingers, getting Butler's attention, and pointed to the watery pool just off the island. "You don't have to do this!"

"I don't. But I'm getting paid an awful lot of money. And I'm tired of talking."

I whistled. Butler stabbed his trunk into the water and snorted, filling his trunk. Then I dove for the dirt as the Sharps rifle thundered. The shot tore into the dirt where I had been standing, casting up a mass of mud and making my ears ring. Thalia screamed and I grabbed her arm and tugged her down—next to the fire.

Butler swung his trunk back and sent out a torrent of swamp water—right onto the blaze. The fire rushed out with a hiss. That blanketed the clearing in darkness and choking white smoke.

Gave us a chance. I pulled Thalia to General Butler and tugged down the rope ladder—knowing where it was by memory, not by sight. Prong might take a shot at Butler, but the flash would reveal his hiding place and it would take more than a rifle round to bring down the General. That gave us a chance.

Thalia went up, carrying Lady with her. My hope was to get everyone aboard and charge out of there, before Prong's eyes could adjust to the dark and he could start picking us off. Unless he decided to walk right in—say hello up close.

More shouts below me. "Get rid of these chains and give me a pistol, Clarke—I'll get him. Cut him down the moment he steps into the clearing." Ginny Wells wanted to help.

"You'd shoot me in the back—first thing. And be quiet, for God's sake!" I whispered up to the howdah. "Thalia, you made it?"

"I think so—whoa!" She let out a squeak and I could make out her dress, white in the moonlight, sliding to the side. Goddamn that dress! Might as well be a marked target for Prong. She was nearly tumbling off, her little horse whickering and making Butler snort and shake his ears. I needed to get up there—but Prong would arrive soon and if he caught me climbing, he wouldn't hesitate.

No noise from the edge of the clearing. No tell-tale crunch of a fallen leaf under Prong's boot. But he was coming—close enough to look his victim in the eye when he pulled the trigger.

I spun around and looked at Wells. Her remaining eye stayed fixed on me, full of fear. But anger too. And she was fine with a gun. I'd seen it before, when we had our first run-in out in the Llano. Maybe if we were firing together, we'd have a chance.

The Hell with it.

I dug into my coat, drew out the key, and tossed it down. "Thank you kindly." She shoved it into the lock and the chains fell to the ground with a rattle. "Now, a pistol."

That's when Prong made his arrival—right in the edge of the clearing. My eyes had adjusted enough to see him, outlined between the trees. He had both hands extended, a revolver in each. Looked a little like one of them living dead men they tell stories about in Gran-Haiti—the zombies. Right down to his dead eyes.

I drew the howdah pistol and fired—one barrel. He fired back, and gun smoke and the echoing roar filled the clearing. Butler trumpeted in pain, trunk flailing, and Thalia screamed. He'd been hit.

The smoke faded. Prong wasn't there. A quick glimpse at the edge of the island showed his coat rustling as he slipped behind a stout swamp tree. He'd moved fast—firing and leaping for cover. He'd be popping out a moment later to finish me.

No time for the spare horse pistol I kept in one of Butler's saddle bags. Instead, I ripped the Cavalry Colt out of the holster on my belt and tossed it down. Wells caught it, and she spun the pistol in the direction of the tree and blazed away, fanning off three shots and keeping him hidden.

Buying us time

I grabbed the rope ladder and went up, the General already shuffling his feet and starting to leave. I made it up to the howdah. Thalia lay there, clutching a saddlebag and trying not to fall off. More gunfire below. Wells screeched.

I reached General Butler's neck and settled into place. Down below, Prong peered out from the tree. I aimed the howdah pistol and fired. The second barrel. The last barrel.

It sundered bark, but did little more.

"Butler—go!" I shouted and he broke into a gallop. "Wells—grab on!"

But she had made it to the mule. She wrenched the hobble free, hopped onto its back, and fired at Prong once more. I was grateful that she'd done that. But then she wheeled the mule away and took off into the swamp. Taking my pistol—and her bounty—away with her.

By then, General Butler had made it to a good pachyderm gallop. He smashed and splashed through the underbrush, making branches rake my back and nearly steal my hat. Poor Thalia held on and I reached back to pull her in the center of the howdah.

We ran into the safety of the swamp.

It was dawn when we left the bayou. I didn't know where—simply green fields, split with creeks, and a little dirt pathway leading into the distance. The sun had come up, and I was swaying in the saddle. Behind me, Thalia had curled up, holding her little horse close, and fallen asleep. I didn't want to wake her.

Prong would be following. He was on foot and we were mammoth-back, so at least that gave us some time. But he'd be coming with Judgement Day-certainty.

We needed to get help. I needed to rest, find out where we were. There was that bullet in Butler's side. Not much more than a gnat's bite to him, but it and the gator bites could get infected and it would have to be dealt with. Then I could hear Thalia's story.

And send her home

She deserved a better guardian than me.

CHAPTER TWO

TRAMPLING OUT THE VINTAGE

It was about midmorning when Thalia awoke. About the time I spotted a town up ahead—a Freedman's Town, judging by the high walls and the Union flag fluttering bold atop the watchtower. Small town and military fortress, all rolled into one. Maybe a little of the latter now. Fields surrounded the town, but they lay overgrown and fallow. These days, no one was cultivating anything. A raven sat on an untended plough wedged in the earth of one such farm, while its friends soared in lazy circles in the cloudless sky.

"Hmmm." Thalia made a little mumbling before sitting up—and almost falling straight off the howdah. Only my arm, thrust back, saved her. Little Lady sprang up and whickered madly, until Thalia hugged her again and set her in her lap. With her knees folded under her skirt and her hat askew, she looked like she was part of a particularly chaotic picnic. "Ah—oh—Mr. Clarke. Thank you."

I touched the brim of my hat and looked ahead. "Obliged."

She watched as I rode on, in silence. "How do you do it? How do you manage a mammoth?"

"It's not that tricky." I patted the bumps of Butler's head. "All in the knees. Mostly, you stay out of the General's way. There's no smarter beast than a mammoth. He'll know what you want even before you do, and he'll work to get it."

She swallowed, suddenly nervous. "Do you suppose—do you suppose I could give it a try?"

I considered it. Well, why not? Wouldn't make our situation any worse. And so I slid back, helped Thalia into position, and let her ride. General Butler walked ahead with the same easy gait. He even raised his trunk up and wrapped it around Thalia in a slithery hug, which made her giggle.

She kept still, perched on Butler's neck like a natural. "So—where's breakfast?"

Breakfast. It would be hardtack and jerky and maybe some apples that I'd kept in the bottom of our saddle bags for over a month—intending to give them to Butler as a treat. Washed down with whiskey, which I kept in ample supply. Not exactly appetizing. And the girl's question did arouse a rumble in my belly.

I pointed ahead. "We'll find something in town."

"And that town is…?"

We reached the entrance. A stout gate, currently open, with the name emblazoned on blue paint above the archway: Jubilee. I'd never heard of it. Two sentries—Colored men—perched above the gate, both armed with long guns and suspicious faces. I gave them a wave with my hat and Thalia made an awkward curtsy from her place on Butler's head. That did little to remove their suspicion, but they didn't shoot at us.

I considered that a fine welcome.

Inside, Jubilee was as neat as a village in a kid's storybook. A little general store, bank, schoolhouse, and an inn and restaurant right at the middle, all freshly-painted and occupied by a couple citizens going about midmorning affairs. Two things were different than most places I've ridden Butler through: everybody was Colored and all of them gave me and Thalia stares like we'd emerged out of a hole in the ground stinking of brimstone. I didn't blame them. Freedman's Towns were having a hell of a time ever since the bluecoats protecting them went away.

We stopped at the inn, which boasted a café on the first floor. I swung down and helped Thalia from her perch. Lady jumped from her arms and ran about, neighing and kicking up her little hooves until Thalia soothed her. That got the attention of everyone from folks heading to the dry goods store to the angels in heaven. So much for being discreet.

I patted Butler's furry flank. "Be good." Then, Thalia and I went in.

Quilts hung up on the walls. Polished tables and fine food—a few people already enjoying a late morning lunch. Thalia and I sat down and she carefully spread out the napkin and tucked it in her collar as I wondered what sort of coffin varnish they had on tap. A young waiter, all awkward, youthful angles, emerged and took our orders—soft-boiled eggs for her, biscuits and gravy for me—and then skedaddled.

"What a charming little place," Thalia said.

"Like a spider's web," I muttered. "Let's just eat and hightail it out of here before the other foot drops."

"I never expected Corporal Clement Clarke to be such a coward." She reached for the water jug the waiter had set on our table. "Now, while we eat, I shall tell you the nature of the wicked conspiracy my father uncovered—which threatens the very fabric of our national character."

"You can tell it all you want," I said. "It still ain't my business and I still don't care."

Then the door slammed open and the other foot dropped. A woman entered, clad in a rumpled Union greatcoat and patched trousers. She looked like some long-legged wading bird, with lean limbs and a swan neck, maneuvering carefully amongst the diners—who had all stopped their eating and gazed at her with a measure of respect and wariness. An old Federal cavalry hat topped her head, with a spray of white feathers in the brim, and she carried the biggest rifle that I had ever seen, complete with a fancy spyglass mounted above the barrel. When she hoisted the rifle up and pointed it straight at me, it looked even bigger.

I clutched my glass. "Howdy." Fear, my constant companion, came rushing back.

"I had my eye on you two since you arrived on that mammoth. Now, state your names. Yours and the girl's."

An alias—that's what we needed. Prong would be on our trail, asking questions, and this riflewoman could easily spill the beans. Just pretend that I was some traveling salesman with his Chinese niece, bound for some distant port. Sure—a traveling salesman with iron on his hip and a Columbian mammoth outside.

"I'm called…" I started.

"This is Corporal Clement Clarke, formerly of the 2nd Elephantine Dragoons." Thalia interrupted me, and even left her chair and executed a curtsy. "I'm Thalia Elizabeth Ridgeway, of the St. Louis Ridgeways. It's a pleasure to make your acquaintance, ma'am."

Miss Markswoman seemed a little taken aback by Thalia's introduction, which was more fitting for a society charity dinner than a talk involving a rifle. She blinked and lowered the gun. "Lenora Hewitt," she explained. "I suppose I'm the unofficial sheriff of Jubilee." At least she wasn't pointing a firearm at me anymore. I let a little breath slip out from between my clenched teeth at that.

The name dredged forth a memory. "Lenora the Lioness?" I couldn't help smiling. "You was with Tubbman, right? Working with her spy ring, feeding us Federals intelligence as we was going South?"

"Did plenty of fighting too," she replied. "But I remember the Elephantine Dragoons. Even worked with some of them, now and then. Never seen so many elephants, all marching together." A tiny curve of her lips. Was that a smile? "But that was a long time ago. What are you doing here now, Corporal?"

Thalia kept on blabbing. "He's assisting me in battling a conspiracy…"

"Hush." I glared at her and she fell silent. Then I looked back. "Look, Miss Hewitt—all due respect to you, I know we're outsiders and this is your town and whatnot—but we got secrets worth keeping."

"All due respect to you, Corporal Clarke, but this town's got troubles, and that means I need to know your secrets. All of them." She whistled. "Maybe I'll show you why I'm called the Lioness and you'll be convinced."

The saloon doors creaked open and saber-tooth padded inside. A massive cat, the mother of all lions and tigers that one might see in a European Zoo. And even for smilodons, this was a large specimen. Massive tawny shoulders, limbs of coiled muscle, a shaggy neck surrounding a huge head that came up to my belly button. There were those saber-teeth, a pair of pale Bowie knives just waiting to slice into flesh. The tabby monstrosity sat on its haunches next to Hewitt, revealing a leather collar with a silver coin bearing the beast's name.

"Say hello, Butterscotch," Hewitt ordered.

A deep rumbling purr. If a volcano could purr, that would be the noise it made.

And yet, the folks eating didn't go running for the doorway in panic. They were frightened, true—but more of me than of the giant killer cat in their restaurant. Perhaps Butterscotch had me beat in the manners department.

The waiter chose that moment to emerge, bearing our breakfasts. The kid took one look at Hewitt and at Butterscotch and started back for the kitchen.

"No, no—it's all right." Hewitt's voice went kind. "Just drop them off. These folks can eat. And tell me their business over breakfast."

He deposited the food. Butterscotch's amber eyes followed the eggs and my mess of biscuits.

"He's gorgeous," Thalia said, clutching Lady close.

"Thank you." Some genuine gratitude from Hewitt. "My old master used to raise them. Fighting cats. Trained from cubhood to battle." Her tone went cold. "They'd never know what it was to be free, until some bigger tiger took out their throat. I stole Butterscotch same day I stole myself, and I've been raising him ever since." She reached out and snagged the fork right from my plate, then skewered a biscuit and pulled it free. Half vanished into her mouth and the other dropped into Butterscotch's maw. Like tossing a pebble into the Grand Canyon. "Now—what are you doing here?"

"I am being pursued by an assassin," Thalia explained. "A fellow named Prong. He killed my father and intends to do the same to me."

"An assassin." Muttered with a mix of disbelief and disgust that such a thing could happen.

"That's about the size of it," I agreed. "I'm taking her to St. Louis, back to be with her folks."

Hewitt sighed. "A child, pursued by a killer. Good Lord." She brushed her temple with her fingers. "I'd offer you sanctuary. Hell, I'd offer to put a bullet through this assassin, or have Butterscotch chew on them some. But we've got troubles enough here in Jubilee, and I cannot extend a charitable hand."

That served me fine. I wasn't inclined to seek charity.

But Thalia listened carefully between dainty bites of eggs. "What sort of troubles?"

"You can imagine." That explained plenty. "It's all cause of Federal troops leaving. The South is officially Reconstructed, Lincoln and Grant are out of office, the Bluecoats have gone home, and all the vipers are slithering out. No one to stop them." A smirk as she scratched Butterscotch behind the ears. "No one but us."

I was curious, considering that I fought a war that ended up setting these folk free and building the Freedman's Towns. "What are you up against?"

"The Paladins of the Pale Petunia." She rolled her eyes. "I know. Redshirts and White Leaguers and Klansmen—all with their silly names and idiot pantomimes. But these clowns are shedding Freedman's blood all over the South. Led by a Georgia bastard named Horace Wick, who's got himself political ambitions. Last month, they hit the Freedman's Town of Liberty. Put it to the torch and butchered everyone who couldn't escape."

Thalia covered her mouth. "Oh God."

"I expect they're coming here next. We're armed and ready." She stared at her boots. "But so were the folk in Liberty."

"We shall assist you in Jubilee's defense." Thalia smiled after the grand announcement and then filled her mouth with eggs.

"What?" I stared at her, gravy dripping on my chin. "Miss Ridgeway, we ain't doing nothing of the sort..."

"We need all the help we can get." Hewitt slung her rifle over her shoulder. "That mammoth of yours, for instance—could give us the edge we need."

"That's too bad, because we ain't helping." By then, my plate was mostly clean. "Miss Ridgeway doesn't know what she's talking about. We're gonna finish our meals, get some provisions, and ride on out of here. On that mammoth."

"What if I don't give you a choice in the matter?"

This was getting bad.

But it didn't bother Thalia. "Well, there's no need." Her eyes flashed. "We are staying and we are helping. They are innocent people, good people, defending themselves against a cruel and villainous pack of butchers. We shall stay and help. I insist upon it."

Hewitt looked at the two of us. "I'll leave you to sort it out. I'll be in the schoolhouse. Turned it into an armory, what with the devil on our doorstep." She snapped her fingers, summoning Butterscotch to his feet. "But you can go ahead and flee, if you want. We're well-used to white folks doing that. Especially after they promise they're gonna help. Either way, the mammoth stays."

I couldn't believe this. I'd come in for biscuits and now Butler had been recruited for a war. "You really gonna pick a fight with me, Miss Hewitt?"

"I've fought scarier." She patted Butterscotch, who let out another dark purr and pushed the door open with his head. Then she stepped back into the sunlight and left.

I looked back at Thalia. A staring contest with an eleven-year-old. I felt about as tall as a tick. "We're leaving. I'm taking you back to your grandparents in St. Louis and then riding General Butler west—no matter what Miss Hewitt or her pet tiger says—and that's all there is to it. I owe your father that much, but no more."

"I'm not leaving."

"I could carry you."

"I'll scream." She set Lady down, and the little horse darted to some fallen gravy and began licking it up. "And I'll fight. I'll bite you, sir. Quite viciously." Was her father this stubborn? I don't remember it being so. Maybe she got it from her ma. "At least go to the schoolhouse. See what they have for their defense. You fought a war for freedom. You can fight one more battle." Then she picked up the spoon and started drumming on the table. Lady whickered and stomped her hooves in time. "*In the beauty of the lilies, Christ was born across the sea—with a glory in his bosom that transfigures you and me.*" She pointed the spoon at me defiantly. "*As he died to make men holy, let us die to make men free! While God is marching on!*"

I took a final bite of the biscuits and reached for the payment—my billfold was getting mighty sparse. "I got no intention of dying."

"Then don't."

I tossed the cash down and stood. "Fine. We'll visit the schoolhouse. If it'll shut you up."

She pantomimed locking her lips and tossing away a key. Thank Christ for small mercies.

It turned out that Hewitt had assembled quite the little arsenal in the schoolhouse. She'd pushed the children's desks to one corner and set rifles and shotguns leaning against the wall emblazoned with number and letter charts and framed photographs of Abraham Lincoln, Frederick Douglas, and the like. The kids had been etching pictures of local animals, and giant armadillos, sloths, and mammoths covered the chalk tablets set on their seats. Quite a few of Butterscotch as well. He currently lay by the teacher's desk, batting a pillow sewn with turkey feathers between his paws.

"Fine. We'll visit the schoolhouse."

Hewitt gestured to the rifles. "Gifts from Gran-Haiti. They've been going to all the Freedman's Towns, dropping off weapons. Had to be quick and skedaddle back to the Free City of New Orleans before they got noticed, but their help is appreciated." She patted a crate set on the teacher's desk, bristling with dynamite. "Even if I couldn't speak the French to express my thanks."

I whistled at the implements of destruction. "You reckon this'll be enough?"

"We don't got men enough to use them all. And plenty of women and kids—who the Pale Paladins will not spare, by the way." She picked up a repeating rifle and gave the lever a test. "I sent word to Colonel Allensworth. He's with a bunch of Longhorn Soldiers on leave from their place in the cavalry. He might rustle a few up, come and help."

"Longhorn Soldiers are good, ma'am. I met a few when I was with the Elephantry out west. Before I mustered out. And I remember Allensworth from the war."

"But will they come in time?" She set down the repeater. "That's the question. And then there's the enemy to consider." She counted on her fingers. "Wick has got a small army. Confederate veterans, most of them, so they've got experience. Old plantation money's bought them a fine arsenal. And rumor has it that Wick has a Hell Pig on his side."

"A Hell Pig?" I asked.

"Entelodont. He raises them on his farm for the meat—fed the meanest boar on alligators and the flesh of slaves, and now rides it around like he's Satan's own horseman." She snorted. "That hog from Hell will be a problem—unless your mammoth's there to stomp it."

So that was why they wanted Butler so badly.

Thalia had stood silently in the corner, holding Lady. She was a tough one, all right. Had to be, traveling halfway across the country after losing her father to seek out an old cuss like me. But standing in that schoolroom, surrounded by weapons, had to make her feel very small. I have to admit, I felt for her—even though her damn fool notion of making me a soldier once again had put me here.

Hewitt snatched up the feather-trimmed pillow and tossed it in the air. "So, that's about the size of it." Butterscotch dove for it, caught it with both paws, and bore it down. "I can use a gunslinger, Corporal. Along with the war mammoth too. No two ways about it."

"You can't have…" I stopped and sighed. Wasn't my fight, simple as that. But then I looked at Thalia's face, and all that expectation that I would do the right thing put a quiver in my breath and a tremor in my heart. I couldn't stand it. "I—I've got to take the air." I put on my hat and brushed through the schoolhouse door. Back into a beautiful afternoon.

I crossed the street and went to General Butler, who had been snacking from an apple barrel the kindly hotel staff had donated. His trunk snaked down, emerged with a treat, and popped it into his mouth as his dark eyes settled on me. Then the trunk wrapped around me in a serpentine embrace—he'd been with me long enough to know when I was feeling low. And I felt low now.

Another battle. I didn't want that. Preferred hunting down outlaws, most of whom—contrary to the dime novels—usually preferred the Alive to Dead option and went willingly soon as you pointed a pistol at them. That was the whole reason I was dragging Thalia back to her grandparents instead of even listening to her damn-fool notion of some grand conspiracy.

But a look at Jubilee told me the cost of my cowardice.

A little over a decade ago, these folks had been in chains. A war had ended it, but even that cataclysm hadn't sapped the need of some Southerners to stay on top. That actor assassin and his compatriots, for instance. Booth had snuck into Ford's Theatre to put a bullet into the president, and it was only Lincoln's beloved pet ground sloth, Cincinnatus, who had saved his life. And poor Secretary Seward and Vice President Johnson, butchered in a sickbed and a street corner, weren't that lucky. Afterwards, Lincoln had given the Freedmen's Bureau all kinds of powers, taking land from the slavers and giving them to the slaves.

But Lincoln was out of office, and so was Grant, and now the Federal troops went home and those slavers came again, wearing masks and giving themselves ridiculous names, to burn and destroy what the Freedmen had built.

Another image came to mind. My father—dangling from a rope after the Missouri Border Ruffians had shot him to death. He and my ma had traveled to Kansas from Illinois, birthed me and started a farm, all to keep the tide of bondage from spreading further west. My father had died for it.

And here I was, fixing to run away.

I hugged General Butler's trunk. "It ain't our fight," I murmured. "It ain't our fight." Maybe if I said it often enough, I'd be convinced.

Then, a familiar caterwauling hit my ears. "Unhand me! Goddamn it—let go! I ain't done nothing wrong!" It was One-Eyed Ginny Wells. I stared down the street as Lenora Hewitt and Thalia, along with Butterscotch, emerged from the schoolhouse. Two of Hewitt's sentries hauled in Ginny Wells, who was hissing and writhing—a prairie cheetah in a trap. They tossed her down in the gravel. Butterscotch arched his back and gave her a growl and Wells growled right back at him.

Lenora let her rifle dip to face Wells. "Good Lord. It's just raining white folks today, ain't it?"

Wells brushed herself up. "Frying pans and fires, that's my goddamn life." She spotted me. "Clarke. What the hell are you doing here?"

"Stopped for a bite to eat," I said. "Hewitt, this here's One-Eyed Ginny Wells. She's an outlaw, and an annoying one at that."

"Hello there, Miss Wells," Thalia said, with customary politeness.

It gave Ginny Wells pause. She stopped her outburst and smoothed back her hair. "Hello there, honey." Then she stood. "I'll tell you my story, then. Might as well. Can't run nowhere—not with the hog from Hell out there." She pointed past the gates. "Soon as I left the swamp, I hit the grasslands and went straight into a group of amateur soldiers. Something between an armed camp and a Sunday picnic. They was snacking on fried chicken and roasted devil pig, liquoring themselves up for battle. Called themselves the Pearlescent Patriots of the Pickled Punk or some such nonsense."

"The Paladins of the Pale Petunia," Hewitt said.

She snapped her fingers. "That's it! Anyhow, they was nice to me for a while. Gave me some food and a little corn liquor and told me I was a fine flower of Southern womanhood. I'm from Missouri, but I accepted the compliment graciously." She whistled. "Then, one of them Pale Paladins recognized me. Seems I robbed his bank back in the day. After that, the smiles went away and the ropes came out. Barely made it out of there with my life."

Hewitt had been listening. "They're following you?"

"Yup. Be here a little before sunset."

"That's it." I turned back to Butler. "Thalia—mount up. We're leaving."

"Once again, I refuse." She had folded her arms. "We shall stay and defend the right."

"Corporal." Hewitt moved in front of me. "If what Miss Wells says is true, the Paladins are close by. They'll have spread out. They surround a settlement before making their attacks. Cut off all escape. You run now, they'll find you in the woods, in the dark. And you know what'll happen."

My father's body, hanging from that rope—riddled with bullet holes. A sign nailed to his belly. 'He Tills the Free Soil in Paradise.' If the Paladins caught me and Thalia in the forest, that's what would happen to us.

"You ain't gotta fight. I won't force you to. But I won't let you flee and risk your lives. Nor the life of that child you're looking after."

Thalia was as happy if she'd found a new puppy under the Christmas Tree. "That settles it. We shall stay and aid in the town's defense."

"*We* ain't doing nothing," I told her. "You're gonna go hide with the women, old folks, and other kids in whatever place is the most secure. The bank vault, I'd say. Butler and I—we'll be the ones fighting." There. I had said it. I stared into the dark eyes of my mammoth, who hadn't asked for this anymore than I had. “We got no choice now.”

“Thanks.” Hewitt offered her hand to Wells. “And Miss Wells, I’ll make you the same offer. You run, the Paladins will probably catch you in the woods. But stay, and we’ll offer protection.”

“Hell with that. Day I hide from a fight is the day I climb into my coffin.” She looked ready to back those words up. “Get me a six-gun and put me on that goddamn wall. Or better yet, get me some dynamite.”

“We got dynamite,” Hewitt said.

“Well now.” A truly frightening grin crossed her face. “Things are looking up already.”

I didn’t share her optimism.

And so the remaining hours passed in a fury of preparation for the battle to come. We didn’t have enough time, nor enough weapons, nor enough men, but we prepared as best as I could. Hewitt placed those who could bear rifles—women and boys little older than Thalia amongst them—on the parapets, while Ginny loaded up a repeating rifle and put a box of dynamite close by. We had the critters—Butler and Butterscotch—wait in an alley behind the gate. Out front, they’d get picked off before they could do any damage. But if the Paladins got through the gate—and with their numbers and armaments, they just might—the beasts could do real damage up close.

Would it last against the Paladins’ onslaught? We could only guess. It was like the times before the battles in the war. You loaded your weapons, tightened the harness on your elephant, and said your prayers. That was it.

Then, before I knew it, the sun had gone down and the warning call came from the watchtower. I was by the bank, setting a bandolier of rifle rounds over my vest. Thalia was helping some of the old folks inside as the shout echoed over Jubilee. She went over to me, her face pale—all the bravado of her good cause vanished.

“Corporal Clarke.” She swallowed. “Please—be careful. I can’t—I can’t lose you.”

I slid the first round into my buffalo rifle. “No promises, Miss Ridgeway. None at all. No go and stay safe yourself.”

She smiled sadly and we went our separate ways.

I headed up the ladder to the battlements and looked out over the stockade. Wells sat on one side, dynamite candle clutched in her fingers while Hewitt brought her marksman’s rifle to her shoulder and snapped open the lid on the mounted spyglass. All around us, the defenders of Jubilee crouched low with their weaponry and waited.

Across from us, torches gleamed. Looked like the stars had descended from the heavens and were rolling their way across the grass. I squinted. About two score of them Paladins, on horse or camel-back, wearing a motley mix of uniforms. Some had old Confederate gray, while others bore civilian clothes. White bands on their arms—but no masks. Out here, there was no need to hide.

Wells struck a match, brilliant in the shadows. "What's going on out there?"

"It's Wick." Hewitt pointed. "He's making a speech."

One hulking beast, bigger than the horses of the Paladins, crossed in front of them. There was Colonel Horace Wick, clad in a black broadcloth coat. He had a stiff Robert E. Lee beard and a top hat. Looked more like he was going to the opera than to battle. And his mount—the Hell Pig. That monster looked like Satan's lapdog, with almost spindly hooves supporting a massive, muscled body, a long tooth-filled snout, and bristly black fur.

Colonel Wick raised a gloved hand. "Men of the South, the time has come!" He rode before the line of Paladins, giving his grand speech. "The Yankees have gone home, and their carpetbagger rule, which would see our homeland turned into Blackest Africa, can now be purged! Let us defend our hearths and homes, our children, our womenfolk—Lord, let us defend our lovely womenfolk..." His booming oration carried out across the plain. This fellow was used to making speeches.

Hewitt put her rifle to her shoulder. "Long-winded bastard."

"Fearless, though," I said.

"Nah. Just stupid. Figures he's out of range." Her tongue poked out of the corner of her mouth as she stared down the rifle. "And maybe he is." She pulled the trigger and the Sharps rifle boomed, the rifle's cry echoing over the darkened fields—an angered animal, keening out a warning. "But maybe he ain't."

Wick's oration ended. He swayed in his saddle, the Hell Pig snorted and wiggling back and forth—and then he drooped.

A roar went up from the Paladins. They charged.

"Winged him." Hewitt put another round in the chamber. "Goddamn it."

"That's all right." I hoisted up my own long arm. "Something tells me you'll get another chance."

The Paladins came rushing in, hoisting up their torches and firing from the saddle. There was that old Rebel Yell, shrill and terrible, coming ahead of them as their shots whistled down into our little ranks. Our rifles clattered away to meet them. Fire split the night and death welled up in the front of the charging column as men and horses vanished under the chatter of lead. The other riflemen cracked away too, and bullets flew back and forth.

I opened fire too, sighting on some pot-bellied defender of Dixie in the same ranks and shooting him right off his horse. A killing shot? I don't know, but he left the saddle as if struck by a ram. I slid in another round and fired again.

The dead lay thick on that grass. Riderless horses ran and camels brayed as bullets sank home. We cut down the Paladins—but then they started getting their shots in. Revolver and carbine cracked, and the defenders of Jubilee died. Hewitt let out a sudden gasp and dropped down, a groove carved in the flesh above her ear. She tore free a handkerchief and knotted it tight around the wound, then rose to fire again.

"Still glad that you stayed put, Miss Wells?" Her rifle roared as the riders neared our gate.

"You kidding? This here's more fun than a Kentucky turkey shoot." She'd touched the fuse to a candle of dynamite, the glow lighting her smile and eye-patch, and then she sent that bomb sailing right into their front ranks.

I ducked, but still caught a wind of heat as the explosion turned night into day. Men and animals and pieces of them both went sailing every which way, and Wells was cackling as she lit another stick of dynamite and sent that whistling down to join its predecessor. The boom came and grass and earth went into the sky and descended in a shower.

Back in the town, General Butler trumpeted. The kind of noise he made when there was fighting to be done. I guess he wanted to join the fun.

Then another explosion thundered to life—but it wasn't Wells' dynamite. The planks of the stockade shook under my boots and I tottered down, falling hard onto my back. I rolled over and looked down. The gate had been blasted open. The Paladins must have brought bombs too, and now they were riding in, putting those torches to use by hurling them into every building.

Thalia was hiding in one of them structures. So were all the Jubilee folk who were too young or too old to defend themselves. But these fine defenders of the south—these Paladins of the Pale Petunia—didn't give a damn about that. They'd ruled an empire of bloodshed for years, and now they'd fight to get it back.

I didn't want that to happen. Old soldier's instincts came rushing back, from when I rode my father's plough mastodon with the Kansas Irregulars all the way to the Elephantine Dragoons. I fired the rifle first, catching a Paladin in the back, and then dropped down, slung the buffalo gun over my shoulder, and went for the howdah pistol and Cavalry Colt in the same moment.

They roared in tandem. I blasted another Paladin from the saddle, his mare galloping past me with his blood down her flank. Another Paladin, a pockmarked fellow who'd put an old bayonet on his rifle came rushing from the side—right in time to catch the second barrel of the howdah pistol. His skull just about vanished as the impact sent him sprawling against the side of the café.

But those were all the rounds I had. Didn't have time to reload as another rider came in—and then what he was riding ploughed straight into me and sent me flying.

The world spun. Fire, night sky, and the oinking, grunting, thrashing form of the Hell Pig. I crashed to the earth a moment later, ribs aching, and breath refusing to make its way into my lungs. All I could do was roll over. There was the Hell Pig, with Horace Wick tall in the saddle. He'd shed his coat and wrapped a bandage about his arm, but the hog was unharmed and hungry.

Wanted to shoot him. Wanted to hit him—but I had neither bullets nor energy.

"A white man?" He cocked an eyebrow. "Odd indeed—but my pig will digest you easily enough."

The Hell Pig raced toward me, those big jaws opening up and sweeping low.

A trumpet stopped it. General Butler came charging out from the corner, trumpeting and waving his tusks. Towered over the Hell Pig the way he towered over most things—though not by as much as I would've liked. It weren't like an elephant and a boar. More like an elephant and a rhinoceros. Only this rhinoceros had a mouth full of nasty teeth, and it lunged out and bit deep into Butler's leg. Same one the Tarasque had gotten.

Butler trumpeted and snorted and tried to break free. Blood coursed from the jaws of the Hell Pig. By then I was on my knees, fumbling with the bullets on my belt. Trying to reload, even if nothing short of a Howitzer seemed capable of stopping the Hell Pig.

Wick swung down from the saddle—his boots settling into the dirt. "A big animal, eh? A veritable pachyderm. It matters little. The hog devours all." Behind him, more horsemen galloped in. I was still trying to stand.

Then little hands grabbed my arm. "Corporal!" No—it was Thalia. She was pulling, tugging me toward the shelter of the boardwalk while the Devil Hog wrestled with Butler and Wick opened fire.

That put some movement in my legs. He'd kill us both. I knew it. And that hog would get to feast when it was over. The pain in my body was nothing compared to the worry for Thalia. I matched her grip, dragging her across that grimy street, and we dove for shelter in the alley. Wick's long-barreled pistol and my Cavalry Colt clattered together—neither of hitting much but dirt and the wall. He advanced.

A roar hit the air. Butterscotch came leaping out the shadows—tawny lightning—and went straight into the Hell Pig. Hard to imagine something that big moving that fast, but that's how cats are, whether they're snoozing in the garden sunlight or hunting buffalo on the prairie. The pig reeled back, letting go of General Butler, snorting as Butterscotch settled on its back, right on the saddle, and put them big fangs to work. Wick spun around, staring in shock at the rivers of blood running down the Hell Pig's face.

He had a half-second to look before Butler's good foot stomped down and shattered that pig's face for good.

"That was—that was my prize boar!" He stared in alarm. "You cannot…"

Another rifle roared and he tumbled back. Lenora Hewitt advanced on from the ruined gate, putting another bullet into her rifle and taking aim. Wick was coughing and writhing and trying to raise his gun hand.

"Miss Ridgeway—avert your eyes!" Hewitt called.

"No…" Wick sputtered the words. "The African—cannot win—it's our home…"

"It's our home now." Hewitt fired again and blasted Wick's skull to pieces.

By then, I was able to stand. Thalia clung to me, shuddering—a baby bird fallen from the nest. She vomited and I held her as the fear and disgust that came from the aftermath of violence hit her with all its fury. She was closing her eyes, but I'm sure she'd seen some of it, and it had to hurt.

Butler padded closer. His trunk snaked down, wrapping around her. Giving her the same sort of comforting hug.

I looked back out of the gate. More gunfire cut on the fields—but coming from the west. They came from men in Union blue—Colored men. The Longhorn Soldiers, named after the Longhorn Giant Buffalo that ruled the plains with their younger counterparts. They'd come as promised, off-duty cavalrymen rallied once again to save Jubilee.

Hewitt watched them with a slow smile as Butterscotch snacked on the fallen Hell Pig. "Colonel Allensworth has arrived."

The Paladins couldn't take an attack from the flank and from the stockade. They'd go riding away—to nurse their wounds and prepare for the next battle.

"Is it—is it over?" Poor Thalia shuddered, still held by Butler.

"It is, Miss Ridgeway," I agreed. "You can rest easy."

She was crying. I sympathized.

The next morning, I rose long after dawn, got dressed, and even washed my face. I'd slept in an actual bed, in one of the rooms of Jubilee's inn, and it was mighty nice. So comfortable that I almost didn't want to leave it. But I was powerfully hungry, and so I put on my Stetson and headed down to the first floor to get some grub.

Thalia sat down, across from Ginny Wells, while Lady munched oats from a little bowl on the floor. Wells and Thalia were working on biscuits, bacon, and flapjacks, and talking amiably. Poor Thalia still looked shocked from last night's battle, but Wells was spinning some tall tales, trying to comfort her. Except, as soon as she spotted me on the stairs, Wells jumped up and ran for the door. Still had a biscuit between her jaws and trailed crumbs as she made it outside, where a horse waited. A show of appreciation from the townsfolk of Jubilee, no doubt. She mounted up and went galloping away.

I descended the stairs and joined Thalia, who stared in alarm at the door. "Are you going to chase after her, then?"

I pulled her plate close and reached for the syrup. "I'm too tired."

"Oh." She dabbed her cheek with a napkin.

"Miss Ridgeway, if you want to tell me about why you sought me out—about this grand conspiracy, I reckon now would be the time." I owed her that much, at least.

Her face brightened. She wet her whistle with orange juice. "I'm glad you asked. Once you understand the danger facing the nation, you will no doubt eagerly offer your help." I let her go right on thinking that. "It started when my father was approached by a man named A.B. Mulberry. Mr. Mulberry is a businessman of sorts. He represents a consortium of railroad men, bankers, that sort of thing. Captains of industry. For the better part of a year, Mr. Mulberry courted my father, in the manner of a devoted suitor."

What did that mean? "To what end?"

"Commerce. Commerce and stability. They envision the United States rising from the chaos of the Civil War to become a true economic powerhouse. The manufacturing of the industrialized North, the agriculture of the South, and the resources of the West, all connected by a vast network of railroads." It was bizarre, hearing a child talking about such things. But she continued. "They'd already arranged for the South to join this network. To do so, they helped President Hayes get elected—through a devil's deal."

I stared at her. "What do you mean?"

"Mulberry told it to my father and he told it to me. You see, the election results were disputed and so Mulberry arranged a compromise. Creating a railroad that would extend through the South—that was part of his deal. A small part, perhaps, compared with a much larger provision: the removal of Federal troops. The end of Reconstruction. And in return…"

"A Republican gets to be in the White House."

Trading away Reconstruction in return for Southern votes. I'd heard rumors, and it was no surprise that they were true. This wasn't the party of Lincoln no more. Stopping the slaveocracy, fighting for the Freedmen—that didn't matter much these days. It was about keeping business happy, moving America forward, and that's what this Mulberry fellow must have wanted. He'd found a willing dance partner, helping arrange this infernal compromise to get his railroad.

"So they got the North and the South. That leaves…"

"The West."

"But that's where their plan will fail."

Railroads were going everywhere these days. If you switched trains enough, you could make it from the Free City of New Orleans across Texas, and then up to California. But the Great Plains remained free of the Iron Elephant, as they called the railway. There'd been talk of running one through them plains—a straight line, from East to West—but that dream had never been realized. One reason why: the Indian Nations would never allow it, and in the west—in the Far West—they still ruled.

It weren't for lack of trying. There'd been several wars against the Natives over the years, and we'd inflicted terrible casualties and scorched many of their villages from the plains. But the Indian Elephantry was the best in the world. The last attempt was a major offensive around Little Big Tusk, trying to open up the Black Hills. It had ended with a whole lot of cavalrymen getting stomped. Poor Colonel Custer had barely made it back alive.

Now, there was an uneasy truce on the plains. Everyone knew that if the US really wanted to, they could wipe out Crazy Horse and Sitting Bull and all the tribes, but it would be a costly campaign that no one wanted.

Except for Mulberry apparently. And these businessmen.

"He wanted my father to—to use his position in the Elephantry to create an incident that would lead to war. An incident of such magnitude that it would lead to a total war and a total destruction of the Plains Tribes." She was staring at her plate, the pancakes growing soggy in the syrup. "He didn't pose it that way. Merely discussed a sort of expedition that would leave Washington with no choice but to dispatch troops—and there are many in the military and the government who long to do so. But my father refused, and then threatened to go to the newspapers and reveal the sordid details." Would Rufus Ridgeway's word would even matter against such a consortium of respectable tycoons and magnates? They must have judged it so. "That's when Mulberry sent for Prong." She stopped. A sudden sob, swallowed quickly.

Poor Thalia had been running ever since.

"I considered contacting you or Colonel Mortimer MacDougal, who holds command in Fort Fielding near the border with the Indian Nations. Both were my father's comrades-in-arms. But you were closer."

I wished she'd gone to MacDougal. Or better still, I wished she'd forgotten about this whole matter, as Prong wished, and gone on with her girlhood.

I swigged some coffee. "Could've still gone after MacDougal, instead of seeking me out in a damn swamp."

"I—I grew fearful. I didn't think I could make it to MacDougal's side. Not with Prong after me. So I sought you out." A small smile reappeared. "Go west with me, Corporal Clarke. Help me stop Mulberry. Help there be peace."

Peace? There'd been blood on the prairie for years, conspiracy or not. Stopping this plot would do little when some fresh spark would set the frontier ablaze sooner or later. And none of it concerned me.

I stood. "Finish your breakfast. Then we'll start back to St. Louis. And that's where I'll leave you." Her grandparents were high society types—even Prong wouldn't dare move against them. His employers wouldn't let him. Hell, Thalia's folks might even be invited to join in the conspiracy.

But my denial didn't feel good to say. I'd let her down, and she didn't even have the energy to argue. I went outside instead, to where Butler waited at the hitching post with his own breakfast. He was munching on heads of cabbage and brushing his trunk over his bandaged leg. I patted his side. "One more stop, General. Then it's back to the road for good."

He made a huffing grunt. Maybe I'd let him down as well.

CHAPTER THREE

THE IRON ELEPHANT

The Reverend Colonel Allen Allensworth himself rode by when Thalia was scrambling up the rope ladder onto Butler's howdah. The chaplain of the Longhorns, who never strayed from battle himself. He had been talking to Lenora Hewitt, discussing the town's repairs and future defenses, before noticing my elephant—rather hard to miss—and striding over. I paused and made a quick salute, which he returned. Still tall and imperious, with his stiff preacher's collar emerging from his Union blue cavalry uniform, he cut the same sort of figure he did when he ministered to the Longhorns out west. I think a fellow like him was never off-duty.

"Odd, to see a Columbian Mammoth this far east." He gave Butler an appraising glance. "Seems as well-fed and happy as when we met out west. How are you, Corporal Clarke?"

"I'll be better, once I get to St. Louis." I pointed to Thalia. "I'm taking her home."

"Hmmm. And then what?"

"Return to my wretched ways." Bounty hunting, gambling, and drinking. I didn't number them. Not to a godly man like the Reverend. "Go West, I expect."

"The rambler's life. A luxury I do not possess." He touched the brim of his military Stetson to Thalia, who had settled down awkwardly on the howdah. "My men will have to muster and return west, to Fort Fielding on the border. Leaving our towns and loved ones behind, with only our fears to accompany us."

"Gives me a mind of that fellow pushes the boulder up the hill, only for it to roll down again once he reaches the peak."

"Sisyphus," Reverend Allensworth said. "An apt comparison. I'm not certain I agree. Perhaps Miss Hewitt and myself cannot make things better. But we can stop them from getting worse." He raised a hand in a farewell. "Maybe you'll join us someday, Corporal Clarke. Like old times."

"Like old times," I repeated. Then I went up the ladder and to my place on Butler's neck. We started off, his heavy feet pounding across the road leading to the gate, past buildings scorched with Southern fire.

Hewitt leaned against such a wall, head bandaged. "Corporal." A curt nod. "I owe you. Send word and Butterscotch and I will come running."

"You don't owe me nothing, Miss Hewitt…"

"Not so. You fought for us. Maybe I'll fight for you, or deliver some other favor." A set in her jaw that might be a smile, or something close to it. "I don't like owing white folks. Or feeling like I'm in their debt."

Arguing with her would be a foolhardy endeavor. "I'll keep it in mind."

"Farewell, Miss Hewitt!" Thalia chirped.

"Farewell, Miss Ridgeway." She waved. "And may good luck ride with you."

That was about it for goodbyes. The children of the town ran alongside us, waving to Thalia and Butler as we departed.

A luxury he did not possess. That's what Reverend Allensworth had said. But he didn't seem envious of my luxuries. I looked back at Thalia, who huddled close with Lady whickering softly in her arms. She wasn't my fight. It wasn't my concern. I told myself that again and again, until we reached the border of St. Louis.

We arrived on a flat-bottomed barge, a vessel with the power to carry a Columbian Mammoth and the speed to bring us up to St. Louis within the space of a day and a half. Habitations weren't much and the vittles were sorrier still. Thalia did not complain. She fed her dawn horse, played with General Butler as he squirted water from his trunk at sailors and folk on the shore, and watched a few giant sloths drinking from the water's edge. No arguments and no tantrums.

I gathered she'd realized their futility.

When we arrived in St. Louis, she even gave me directions to her grandparents' manor, and we clambered aboard the General and set off into the city. I even let her play mahout and ride. We had arrived in the early afternoon, and a cool wind came off the river and rustled its way through the cluttered town. The gateway to the West, alive with parties of travelers preparing for the grand exodus. It seemed there wasn't one thoroughfare that wasn't packed with wagons, horses, and camels, nor a moment not split by some beast's bellow or loud conversation.

That faded as we neared the more refined neighborhoods, a little closer to the river. Soon, Butler padded along clean cobblestone streets, occupied only by the occasional stately wagon. Mansion houses loomed behind tall and spiky gates, with wide lawns and grand shade trees. A world of peace and politeness. Far from any I'd ever seen. But this was where Thalia had grown up.

"You're awful quiet," I told Thalia. "Figured you'd be caterwauling."

"It would be a waste of breath, sir." She held Lady close. "I shall find another way west. Seek out someone else."

"And it's good that you do," I agreed. "Be a fine thing, to be rid of you. Reckon I'll get drunk. Can't do that in the company of a child. Yes, sir—I shall get a bottle for me and a barrel for General Butler and we'll both drink ourselves senseless." Maybe I was waiting for her responses. But there was no comment at all.

Then we reached her house, a mansion of grim grey with a backyard leading into the hills. I descended and helped Thalia down, and then we knocked on the door. A butler emerged, with a face like a sun-dried buffalo chip. He looked at me and then at Thalia with the same distaste. For me, that was reasonable. But Thalia? She'd spent her whole life in this house. Where was the affection?

A slight sniff was all the recognition he gave her, and then he looked at me. "I shall fetch Master Hamish and Mistress Mary." His eyes flicked to me. "And whom shall I say has returned our Miss Ridgeway?"

"Corporal Clement Clarke, friend," I said.

"Indeed." He closed the door and shuffled away.

"Sour fellow," I said.

"You don't know the half of it," Thalia muttered.

We waited for a few moments and then the door opened again. The butler brought us into a parlor. The curtains had been drawn, even though there was

"I will fetch Master Hamish..."

plenty of daylight outside, and they kept candles and gaslights going to fight back the shadows. Everything was entirely too clean, tasting of harsh soap. The butler made to take my coat and hat, and then thought better of it and retracted his gloved hands. More footsteps came down the dark hall, and then Thalia's grandpappy and grandma emerged.

They looked a little like her, and more like Rufus. Grandpa Hamish had the same high forehead and the same rectangular sideburns—the only hair that adorned his head. Grandma Mary had something of her granddaughter's round face, though hers was wedged into a perpetual frown. Both wore black, as if in mourning.

Mary took a single step toward Thalia. "Wicked girl! Willful girl!" She pointed to the stairs. "To your room, at once! You shall receive no supper. You will be confined to your chamber until it pleases me to see you released."

She took a step toward the stair and looked back at me. "Goodbye, Corporal…"

"At once!" Mary repeated and Thalia hurried up, Lady galloping along with her.

I still had my hand raised in farewell. My heart pounding and heavy to see such cruelty.

Grandpa Hamish looked me over. "So, she ran to you, eh?"

"Yes, sir. Found me in New Orleans." How much did they know, concerning the conspiracy that had cost their son his life? "It's a cruel world for a child to be in, all alone like that. She handled herself well enough, I should say."

"Hmmm." He squinted at me. "You'll want a reward, I expect."

I shrugged. "One wouldn't go amiss." And my pockets were looking quite empty—so why was I feeling so damnably low? "Sir, I wonder if you know the reason why she found me? I'm a friend of your son, you see. We were in the 2nd Dragoons together."

"Rufus." Mary screwed up her face in a scowl. "We miss him dreadfully—but he is with the angels now. I still keep his letters from the war."

He'd only sent them the one letter, as far as I remember. They'd tried to keep him out of the war. Even paid the fee to get another to enlist in his place, so that he'd reject to call to arms and follow his father into business.

She forced on an expression that might be taken for kind. From a distance. "And you've returned his daughter to us. We are quite grateful." Grateful she didn't cause them more scandal. A Chinese girl, born to folks like this? They'd keep her stuffed away somewhere the neighbors couldn't see.

"Mary." Hamish raised his voice. "Enough." She fell silent. He had extracted his billfold and counted out a number of bills, then held them out at me like some sort of shield. "Will this be sufficient?"

It was double what I'd get for a good bounty. "Yes, sir. Obliged to you." I took the cash and pocketed it. "Did your granddaughter explain why she fled? This notion of hers, considering a conspiracy that had, ah, victimized poor Rufus?"

"She did," Hamish agreed. "The poor girl. The death—it must have shocked her terribly, to make her say such things."

"It ain't true, is it?"

He stared back. "I thank you, sir, for returning our granddaughter. Now, you may go."

I wasn't inclined to stay where I wasn't wanted. I touched the brim of my Stetson to the old folks and went outside. That cash weighed heavily in my pocket. A good amount, for dispensing of some trouble. Now, this chapter was done with and I could go on. Time for the drink that I'd promised myself and to forget all my troubles.

Bet that's what Judas told himself, when thirty pieces of silver jingled in his pockets.

I rode Butler back to the river. His trunk reached up, giving my cheek a pat, and sniffing around. Looking for Thalia, no doubt. Well, I'd get him some grub, and the same for me, and then he'd stop looking. An inn facing the water appeared to be doing a good trade— a two-story structure called the Commodious Camel. As long as they poured whiskey, could grill a steak, and fill a barrel with apples for General Butler, it was the perfect place.

Out front, another mammoth waited on a hitching post. This was a Pygmy Mammoth, imported from California. They raised them in herds out there. He was about the size of a horse, with sandy fur and a fancy collar. The coach next to him, however, was truly odd. Painted dark blue, with a mass of fancy stars and moons and lettering in a language I couldn't understand below 'Ambulatory Arcanum' in gold letters. Some sort of traveling sideshow, perhaps.

I had General Butler stand next to the pygmy and they stared at each other. "There you are." I grinned at him. "You can make a new friend."

Butler trumpeted at the pygmy in response, who flapped his ears and stood his ground. Brave little fellow.

Then I went inside and sat down. I waved some of the bills that Mr. Ridgeway had given me and had a waiter bring me a glass of beer and a steak to go with it, then sent him to ransack his kitchen for enough to feed General Butler. Got a room for the night as well, and even a slice of pumpkin pie for dessert. I dined heartily, sawing at the steak and tucking in as the sun settled into the distance and painted the river gold. The inn's common room was dark and quiet, with a game of billiards clacking away in the corner and a few customers smoking and drinking.

After I'd finished my steak and got my pie, I received a companion. Two of them, in fact—a man and a boy. The fellow was a lean sort in a fantastic costume: a suit and waistcoat of dark blue with a sort of opera cape, a matching bowtie and a fez featuring some wild silver design. A boy of around eight or nine, similarly dressed and with exceedingly bright blue eyes, stood next to him, fiddling with his necktie. He bore a strange hat as well, a little circle of silk.

"Good evening, sir." The gent pulled back the empty chair and sat down without being asked. "I am Professor Alexander Ashe. Delighted to make your acquaintance. Maximilian, cigars for myself for my new friend." The boy skipped to attention, drawing a case from his coat and taking out a pair of Havanas. He nearly upended the whole box before dropping the two on my table. The professor didn't skip a beat. "I take it that is your mammoth out there?"

"That's right," I said. "What's this about?" Thought I already had a feeling.

"A fine animal. And I bet you only want the best for such a magnificent beast." He drew a bottle from his coat—dark green, and with a greenish liquid inside. "I present the Elohim Elixir. I am a Hebrew, you see, and in touch with the ancient biblical spirits of my people. They showed me ancient texts which allowed me to craft this wonderful liquid. It promotes excellent digestion in men and mammoth, cures ailments ranging from shingles to…"

"Not interested."

He snapped his fingers. "Are you certain? Look at my darling nephew, poor little Maximilian. Do you see the way he limps?"

"Drat—my poor leg." Maximilian made his leg twist—but he was a terrible actor. However, he gave me such a pleading, hopeful look that I couldn't help but chuckle. "You sure you don't want to buy some, sir? It is fairly tasty."

"He said no, didn't he?" A booming voice from the billiards game. "And when Clement Clarke says something, he means it."

A giant emerged from the shadows—a giant in size as well as reputation. The boy let out a little gasp, and I grinned at the recognition. James Butler Hickok. Wild Bill Hickok. In the flesh. He wore his famed hair long and perfumed, matching his great drooping moustache, and a brilliantly checkered vest and set of trousers below a swallow-tailed coat. His famed pistols rested in a scarlet sash on his hips.

"Oh—oh my." Maximilian smiled suddenly. "Wild Bill Hickok! I've read of your adventures, sir. I've read Romance of the Prairies, and Wild Bill and

Buffalo Bill against the Badlands Banditti, and…"

"I don't give a good goddamn." Hickok grabbed Professor Ashe by the shoulder and hauled him from his chair. "Peddle your snake oil elsewhere and let me dine with my friend or I'll orphan your son right here. Leave the cigarillos. You got that?"

"He is my n-nephew," the professor murmured—before scrambling away. Maximilian wished to stay, but Professor Ashe fairly dragged him into the next room.

Wild Bill sat across from me and I shook his hand. "How are you, Bill? It's been too long."

"That it has, Clem." He selected one of the cigars and sniffed it. "That it has. How's the General?"

"He'll be happy to see you." I tossed him a match. "Surprising, I must say, to find you so far east."

"Oh, not so surprising. You still bounty hunting? Well, I tried my hand at another trade." He struck the match on the table and lit his cigar. "The theatre. Yeah—Cody introduced me to it." William Cody—him and Wild Bill had done some scouting and shooting buffalo for provisions after the Civil War, during the year or so when I was an Indian Fighter. "You get some fellow to write a story, though you ain't really gotta memorize the lines, and then you go up on a stage and folks listen to you talk. I tell you, Clem, they've got a powerful hunger for the West in those big cities."

"Make good money doing that?"

"Enough." He shrugged. "But I don't like all them folk staring at me, and the lights shining so bright. So I said goodbye to Cody and his troupe and tried something else. Got me a Short-Faced Bear, some trained monkeys, and an opera singer, and went to Niagara Falls. Figured I'd exhibit the animals, tell some stories, bring in an audience."

From his tone, I judged it didn't go well.

"Damn bear escaped. Monkeys went crazy. I had to help hunt them down and it's a miracle no one got killed and I didn't get arrested." He stared at the burning edge of his cigarillo. "Another failure."

"You oughtn't to say that, Wild Bill."

"Why shouldn't I? About all I'm good at is drawing a Colt and putting a bullet through someone. And lately, I been feeling like that'll end too." He paused, watching the little flame dance and the trail of smoke. "I feel as if I am living on borrowed time. That I should have perished in some gun battle years ago, or fallen victim to an assassin—shot in the back without warning. Now, I keep breathing, and gambling, and getting into fights, and waiting for that final slug to come."

It was a grim thing to say, and Bill certainly sounded grim when he said it. "I suppose I feel something similar." The words left me with a sigh. "Surviving the war, and then bounty hunting. Playing the tumbleweed ever since." I emptied the beer glass. "Then this girl found me."

"Oh?" He arched a shaggy eyebrow.

"Aw...hell—no. She ain't but eleven years of age. But she was in danger and I got her out of that."

"Playing Galahad?" A chortle of amusement.

"Not quite. I just dropped her back at her house—the little runaway—where's she's despised."

"Break her out, then." Wild Bill grinned. "Burn that house down. Anyone gets in the way, you smack on the head with the butt of your revolver. Or Hell, let Butler sit on them. That'll change their mind." He straightened up. "This little lady—happen to make any enemies during her rescue?"

"Plenty."

"They dress in black? Because two who do have been staring at you since I joined you."

I turned around. Two men had entered the Commodious Camel. Both indeed dressed in black, with bowler hats and crimson ties. They were nearly reflections. Even their facial hair—handlebar moustaches—matched. Same with the irons on their hips. I spun my chair, unbuttoning my shearling vest to reveal the Colt, while gripping the howdah pistol on my waist. For a while, no one said much.

Professor Ashe made an advance on the two from the flank, hoisting up a bottle of Elohim Elixir. "Gentlemen, do you by chance have the Piles? A drop or two of this wonderful liquid will—" The dark-moustache fellow gave the professor a swift cuffing that sent him sprawling on the carpet next to poor Maximilian.

"You're Clement Clarke?" he asked. "My name's Whittaker. We're from the Bracewell Detective Agency." Bracewells. I should've known.

"That a fact?" I asked.

"We'd like you to come with us," his pal said. "To meet with our employer."

Why did they want me to meet their boss? Was that Mulberry? It might be foolish to go with them, but I had to know—especially to see if Mulberry considered me a threat. Or if he still thought the same of Thalia. Maybe I could convince him to cast aside Prong. Make sure the girl was safe.

Hickok flicked his cigarillo in their direction. It skittered across the floor, trailing ash and smoke. "What do you think, Clem? Can I get them both before they clear holster?"

"Easy, Wild Bill." I waved him down. "I ought to go with them. Figure out how things stand. No need for bloodshed." I smiled. "Promise." Outside, General Butler watched through the window. "But there is something you can do for me: look after Butler. Make sure he finishes his meal and get him a barrel of whiskey for the evening. That'll help him sleep."

"I'm no mammoth nursemaid," he replied.

"You'll be fine." I stood and approached the Bracewell boys. "And you two—let's go."

They had a carriage outside. Neither said a word during the whole journey.

The carriage brought us to the railyard, where a private train lurked amongst the silent locomotives and compartments. The Bracewell Boys marched me over, one on each flank. We passed the silent shadowed cars—giant segmented snakes frozen in mid-coil. The Iron Elephant—that was the name the popular press had given to these vehicles, which branded the continent with their heavy tread in the form of crisscrossing tracks. They didn't look much like elephants to me. Didn't look like anything living at all.

One compartment had lights, gleaming through frosted glass windows. This car had been done in rich ochre, the brass around the windows covered in fancy filigree. The whole thing looked like a cuspidor you'd find in a gentleman's club, set on its side and put on rails.

And who should be sitting on the step, working on his pipe, but Orrin Prong?

He gave me a long look as the Bracewell detectives and I walked over. Piano music tinkled away from inside. "Howdy." Prong wreathed his face in smoke. "He's waiting for you."

"I'm waiting for you, friend," I said. "Eager to pay you back, for taking a shot at me in the swamp." False courage—none of us would have a gunfight here. But I had to say something—especially because it seemed he was waiting for his employer's say-so to go after Thalia.

"That weren't nothing personal."

"Got the feeling nothing's personal with you, Prong."

He stood. "Take his irons and let him in to see Mulberry."

Whittaker stood in front of me. "Gotta be done, sir. Hand over those pistols and head on in."

I considered it. Going in unarmed could be dangerous, but if I didn't hand over those guns, Prong and the Bracewell goons could draw on me right there. I was pretty handy. Could probably take the two. But not Prong. Besides, I had no truck with this Mulberry in the first place. I just wanted to let him know that, ensure that Thalia would be safe, and go on my way. So what was the harm? I hauled out the Colt revolver and howdah pistol both.

I've had better ideas.

Whittaker took them and Prong stood aside. He pointed to the steps.

I went in. Soft lights and plush velvet. A full desk in one corner and a full piano in the other, where a fancy-looking fellow played. He wore a smoking jacket of the same crushed red velvet as his furnishings. His fingers worked fast, dancing up and down the keys in careful sequence, and he didn't look up at me as I walked inside. When he did, he kept playing.

"Do you know Mozart, Corporal?"

I went to the side to get a better look at him. A straw-colored goatee and hair split down the middle. Made him look like a music hall devil. I decided to poke a little fun at him. "How about 'Mammoth Maids,' you know that one?" I sang the chorus, to maybe help his memory. "Mammoth Maids won't you come out tonight, come out tonight, and dance by the light of the moon?"

He simply smiled. "Charming. I'm Aloysius Ballard Mulberry. At your service." He lifted one hand from the piano, the other still dancing on the keys, and snapped his fingers. "Now, correct me if I speak falsely, but you seem to be the sort of fellow who pulls a cork. Do you enjoy a bottle, now and then?"

"You speak the truth. You got a cork worth pulling?"

His smile grew. "I must thank you, corporal, for providing me the excuse I needed to open this beauty." He finally stopped playing and went to a cabinet in the corner. "Bourbon—my weakness." He came back with a bottle and a pair of polished glasses. "This bottle is a gift from Jay Gould. Do you know who that is?"

"I've heard the name."

"You've heard the name." He let out a little titter. "Played bridge with him, perhaps? Hah—a jest, my good man. Only a jest." He poured a little glass for me and took another, then returned to the piano. "I'll be honest with you, Corporal Clarke—you have been thrown into a game in which you do not know the rules. It's not your fault, of course. One is not born into an understanding of the delicate interplay of power and economics. One must be taught. In settings academic and practical, one must learn how the world is to be managed. Where did you go to school?"

"Mrs. Lemon's Schoolhouse, down the road from my parents' farm in Kansas. She paddled me once on account I farted during ciphering practice." I drained my glass. It tasted nice—unlike Mulberry. "Mr. Mulberry, let me say my piece."

"Please."

"I don't care what you're doing. I care about Rufus Ridgeway, but he was a grown man and he made his own choices. The daughter, though—I care about her. I want you to know that I'm not a threat and neither is she. Leave us be and go and run your business."

He listened carefully, then bounced his finger off the keys. Played the same note over and over again. "I want to believe you. I truly do. But you strike me as a man with a short temper. Would that be a fair assessment?"

"I'm mild as a lamb, Mr. Mulberry."

"Let us have an experiment." He leaned back. "Do you have any idea why I wish war with the Indian Nations?"

"I'm telling you, I don't care…"

"I want their race exterminated." He said it like he was ordering a plate of oysters and kept playing that note. "The Negro may suffer under the lash of a resurgent south or not, I do not care. But the Indian must go. Now, I'll have you know that I bear the Red Man no malice. In fact, I rather admire his tenacity. But they must be wiped out."

I tried to keep calm. To look him in the eye as he talked of cataclysms and fathomless death.

"And the same with the great animals of the West. The longhorn bison, the great sloth, the Smilodon and dire wolf, and yes, the mammoth as well. A few may be permitted to survive as curiosities in a circus or a zoo, but the vast majority of them should wade into extinction."

Those animals and all their grandeur—gone? It hurt to even consider it, and yet hunting had already done much damage and would do still more.

He touched his temple. "Do you know why?"

Arrogance. It filled him like wine fills a bottle. He had been lording his fancy ways over me ever since I came in and now he was talking about ripping the world apart, for no reason I could fathom. Money? Seems like he weren't hurting for that at all.

I didn't answer his question.

"Because I see a different west, and they have no place in it. Vast networks of peaceful towns, connected by the Iron Elephant—the railroad. Commerce stretching uninterrupted from sea to shining sea. The East, West, and South, united at last into a peaceful world of endless invention and opportunity. To build such a future, all that is unmanageable must be done away with. And it will take a war, you know. A brutal war, to wipe out the Indian Nations so we might fill their lands with railroads and towns and civilization. But a necessary one."

He wouldn't have to fight it. His kind never did. He talked it about like he was ordering dinner, all while pounding that same note. The chime came again and again and again, while he stared at me and smiled.

"And you know what? Your kind—rough-hewn desperados—should become extinct as well." He brought up the glass. "Will you drink with me to that, Corporal Clarke?" He pressed down the key one more time.

I sprang on him. Grabbed his head and slammed it against the piano keys. Played my own little song and put blood on the ivories. I pulled back his head again for another slam, when something heavy connected with mine. I dropped to the carpet and a boot went into my ribs. It was Prong, backed up by the two Bracewell detectives. They dragged me back, kicked me a few more times, and pointed pistols at me.

The world spun and ached. Just forcing breath into my lungs became a battle. Standing up was an impossibility.

"It is as I thought. Very predictable. Very predictable indeed—though you did hit harder than I thought you would." Mulberry loomed over me and wiped his face with a silk handkerchief. "You are a desperado, Corporal Clarke. You are a man of violence. If I let you live, you will come back to vex me in the future. I cannot allow that. And the fact that the Ridgeway Girl was resourceful enough to enlist other to her cause means that she also must be dealt with."

He'd played me like his piano and I'd fallen for it. "No!" The word came out of as a groan.

"Mr. Prong, burn down the Ridgeway Girl's house. Her family's standings are lowly indeed, and there will be no consequences—especially since such accidental fires occur all the time. Make sure she's inside at the time, of course." He drew the handkerchief away, examining the red stain. "Mr. Whittaker, you and Mr. Hackford execute Corporal Clarke and dispose of the body."

Whittaker pulled back the hammer of his six-gun.

"Not here! Dear God." Mulberry waved to the window. "Take him out to the field or something. Deal with it out of my sight."

I tried mumbling out a plea for Thalia. Tried struggling as well. It didn't work. Whittaker and Hackford hauled me out while Prong stepped ahead of them, going to a black horse hitched up behind the compartment. They dragged me past the trains, the Iron Elephants watching me with their dead eyes as I went to my death.

They brought me to a hillock overlooking the railyard. The trains sprawled into the distance and beyond that, the city of St. Louis winked its many lights at the river. I caught glimpses of it as they tossed me down. Whittaker dug his hand into my vest and pulled free my billfold, and let out a little whistle as he snatched my roll.

"Damn vulture," Hackford replied.

"He won't be needing it." Whittaker pulled his revolver and gave it a spin. "Besides, you never know what you're gonna find. You recall that Irishman in Chicago? Had him a fancy necklace of pure silver on him. Fetched a pretty penny."

"Like we ain't getting paid enough." Hackford nodded to the gun. "Go on. Before his strength comes back."

He leveled the pistol at me. Time seemed to slow from a gallop to a trot.

I'd been in positions like this before—more times than I can count. Most were because of my own stupid decisions. Leaving my family home to join the Kansas Irregulars, the craziest bunch of Free State desperadoes after John Brown, and charging my pappy's plough-mammoth straight into a Border Ruffian fort. That terrible charge in the Battle of Blood River Ridge. And plenty of times when I went after outlaws who were a bit too much for me. All my fault, and looking down the barrel of a gun gave me plenty of times to consider my failings.

This time, another feeling came to mind: Thalia. She was in danger. And she had no one to protect her.

A revolver boomed. But no bullet tore into me. Instead, Whittaker spun to the side, his bowler hat coming free as his legs folded. He dropped next to me. Hackford went for his own gun. Another shot punched into his belly before he could clear holster. He dropped low, gasping and clutching at his gut.

Wild Bill Hickok ambled up the hill. "Was aiming for the head." Amusement in his voice. "I can tell myself it's the darkness, that made me miss. A preferable alternative to the simple fact that I am growing old." He fired again. This time, his shot did rip into Hackford's head and drop him next to his fellow. "There we are." He spun both pistols around and put them back in his sash. "Can you stand, Clarke?"

I made it to a crouch and crept over to the Bracewell men. Recovered my pistols and my billfold. By then, the air had mostly returned to my lungs and I could stand up—but the bruises were starting to purple and they'd be sore tomorrow. Added to what I'd gotten in Jubilee, which were just starting to fade.

"Thank you."

"Ah, it ain't nothing." Hickok took my arm and got me on my feet. "You're a friend, Clarke. Not many still living whom I would christen as such." He waved to the base of hill. "Got your mammoth down by some old buildings down there. Best hop on him and ride away. In my experience, Bracewell

Detectives travel in packs."

True enough. But I had something else I needed to do. "The girl. The little one I told you about—Orrin Prong's going to collect her head."

"Ah, Hell." Hickok spat on the ground. "We'd better get moving. Prong's good."

"Better than you?"

He gave me a grin as we headed down the hill. "Ain't a man alive who's as good as me."

We reached General Butler. He knew something was wrong right off, and swept me up with his trunk. Nearly lifting me off the ground. I hugged him back and then went up onto his neck. Butler grunted and snorted, flapping his ears and giving the ground a stomp. "Easy there." I patted his head. "We still got time." Though I didn't know the truth of the matter. Hickok joined me, clearly uncomfortable. He never liked sitting in a howdah. Then we settled off.

A quiet jaunt through the streets of St. Louis, now empty apart from river mist and the occasional late-night carriage rolling to its destination. We left the riverfront and went back to the fine neighborhood, out by the hills. I remembered the way, and so did General Butler. There was dark smoke reaching into the air, and another blaze in my guts. Told myself the smoke, could have some other source—but I knew the truth. When we turned the corner, it became clear enough what had happened to Thalia's manor.

In the time it took for them Bracewell boys to carry me away, Wild Bill to save me, and both of us to get back here, someone had turned it into a torch.

Butler broke into a run, trumpeting as he hurried across the street. Some neighbors had emerged, all in their nightgowns and sleeping caps, and watched the growing inferno that had consumed the Ridgeway's mansion. Fire licked up from the first floor, dancing up the walls and painting the sky with greasy waves of smoke.

It hadn't been burning long. Prong had probably smashed a few oil lamps and dropped a match. But it would be burning down to the foundations, no matter what the firemen did, and everyone inside would go up with it.

No sign of Thalia.

I scrambled down from General Butler's neck and started toward the house—stumbling a little as I went. "Thalia!" I called out her name. It dragged up from my throat like a knife pulled from a stab wound. I could go in. Find the girl—save her.

"Clarke—careful there!" Hickok tried to come after me, and nearly toppled from the howdah. "Damnation—where's that confounded ladder? There." He sent the rope ladder dancing down.

By then, I'd reached the gate and pushed it open. "Thalia!" I shouted for her again.

Footsteps in the yard, mixed with tiny hoofbeats. Lady came running out, eyes white and nostrils flared. Thalia hastened after her. Unharmed, alive, and garbed for the wilderness in a riding dress and a dark coat, complete with boots, not to mention a tailored broad-brimmed hat of dark navy shielding her face.

She went into my arms. "You're all right?" Smudges of ash against her pale cheeks, and she trembled—but no wounds. "Prong—he didn't..."

"I've been in the backyard," she explained. "That assassin broke the windows and set about making his fire. A constable came making his rounds and so Prong set the blaze and fled swiftly—pure good luck. I opened the back door—let out the servants—and retired to my tent." She offered a shy smile. "I judged that was a wise tactic."

"Wise," I said. "It saved your life. And Prong might be lurking around still—meaning we got to go." Another thought. "Your grandparents?"

"They're attending some society function. They left me, locked in my room."

"And why weren't you in there?"

"I escaped."

Lord, she was resourceful. I couldn't help smiling as I stepped back and we watched the house burn. Something inside collapsed, sending up more gouts of flame and another burst of smoke. Hickok joined us, his hat in his hand.

I needed to make some introductions. "Thalia Ridgeway, this is James Butler Hickok."

"Wild Bill," he corrected.

Her mouth opened. "My word. I've read—I've read so many of your prairie romances, Mr. Hickok. I've thrilled to your adventures, and..."

"Clarke, we need to make some tracks." Hickok waved back to the hills. "By now, that fancy pants railroad man will have discovered my handiwork. He'll probably send more Bracewell boys over here—expecting that's where you're heading. You need to leave town. Go west. And you know he'll send some folks over to watch the western routes and a mammoth does tend to stick out."

A fair consideration. "You take Butler, then. We'll meet up later."

"Where?"

I knew the answer. "Grasping Trunk. In the Kansas Territory."

"I know it," Hickok agreed. "A day's ride or so from here."

Thalia had been listening carefully. She had to be wondering what came next—and if I would help her, would answer her request and do anything to battle the conspiracy represented by Mulberry. "How are we to get there, Corporal?" She posed it carefully. "With Mulberry's hirelings watching the borders of the city?" That was all she brought up—nothing about her wild crusade.

A notion occurred—a means to escape, secretly, in a way that Mulberry, Prong, and their whole crew wouldn't recognize.

"Come with me," I said. "We've got to make some new friends."

While Hickok took Butler out of town—perched nervously on the mammoth's back—Thalia and I returned to the Commodious Camel. It was getting to be late, and I feared that snake oil peddler and his boy would be tucked away and asleep. Instead, I found the Hebrew and his fez alone in the common room, lost in a card game. His nephew slumbered on a couch by the window, a dime novel lying half-open on his belly. And who was Professor Ashe playing? None other than the white-suited cardsharp from New Orleans, Mr. Xavier St. James.

He squinted at me as I walked over, the floorboards creaking with my every step. "Ah, hello there—are we—sir, what are you…" Then he recognized me.

"Game's over, friend," I pulled the howdah pistol and slammed it down first, angling both barrels right at his belly. "Unless you want to deal me in."

He stammered, his hand drifting to sweep his mass of dollars and coins—a castle, compared to Professor Ashe's cottage—into his pockets. Then he scrambled away, nearly upsetting the chair, and vanished from the common room.

"Corporal Clarke!" Professor Ashe stared at me as he gathered his winnings—enriched with what he had just lost. "I was going to earn every cent back. I am rather glad—not to mention surprised—to find you intervening on my behalf, but…"

"I'm afraid we don't got the time for cards." I motioned to Thalia, who approached and gave a curtsy. "This here's Thalia Ridgeway. Thalia, say howdy to Professor Ashe."

"How do you do?" She curtsied.

"How do you do?" Ashe repeated, with the same formality. He gave his nephew a nudge with a loafer, startling the boy to surprised wakefulness. "Corporal, what exactly is the meaning of…"

"We need your cart—the fancy one with the moons and stars and whatnot. You're gonna take me and Miss Ridgeway west, to Kansas. Drop us off in a town called Grasping Trunk. Then you're free to go." I didn't say that he had

"We've got to make some new friends."

a choice in the matter, because he didn't. My howdah pistol remained on the table, proving that point.

Young Maximilian beamed at Lady, who trotted close to Thalia's side. "Is that a dawn horse?"

"Yes," Thalia agreed. "Her name is Lady. She can do all manner of tricks."

"My uncle and I have a pygmy mammoth named Goliath. He mostly just eats hay and demands scratches behind his ears." He leaned closer. "Can I see one of the tricks?"

Thalia held her fingers above Lady's head and snapped them. The horse waved her forelegs in the air, clattering back on forth on her hooves in a bizarre little jig. Maximilian was mesmerized.

His uncle looked much more worried, his eyes drifting to the howdah pistol still in my hand. "Must we leave now? I have not yet tapped the market of this fine city."

"We're leaving now," I replied. "Thalia and I will go in the wagon. You and your boy ride up front. Watch for men in dark topcoats and bowlers or a fellow who looks like a vulture without feathers. They show up, give your cart a knock and then run."

He stood slowly. A stoop appeared in his neck, and he looked even more ridiculous in his magician get-up. Judging by the ease in which he sank into the slouching posture, I gathered he'd been in situations like this before. "*Boychick*." His accent changed completely, the refined tones replaced with something from a New York street corner. "Go. Get Goliath ready, Max." He raised his voice. "*Move*!"

Maximilian darted out, clearly worried.

Well, let the boy be scared. There was worse out there than me and Thalia.

CHAPTER FOUR

BURIED BONES

We rode out of St. Louis that very night. Thalia and I were folded up inside Professor Ashe's rolling medicine show—or Ambulatory Arcanum, as he called it. It wasn't exactly comfortable. Rows of his particular panacea, the Elohim Elixir, lined the walls, and they clinked as the wagon rolled along and caught bits of moonlight creeping through gaps in the ceilings and walls that painted everything inside the same sickly bottle green. A little pallet, like something you'd make out of a shelf to hold a kitten, rested in the corner. Probably what passed for young Maximilian Ashe's bedroom. Thalia took that, Lady curled up next to her. She tried to stay up, but fear and desperation can deal fatigue to even the strongest.

She slept soon.

I took the other corner, using my shearling vest as a pillow. Thalia snoozed peacefully—safe, in the knowledge that I was looking after her. A girl who escaped her prison with nothing but gumption and know-how, and went back to a burning house to rescue those inside. By God, I could imagine that Rufus Ridgeway had been proud of her, and for good reason.

By and by, I slumbered too. Too tired for dreams.

Sunlight woke me. Peeking through cracks in the wagon and playing on my eyes. No squeaking of hinges or rumble of wheels against the earth. We had stopped. I sat up and looked at Thalia, who was murmuring and fending off Lady's tongue as the horse stirred her up. Then the wagon doors opened. I drew revolver and howdah pistol both.

Only Professor Ashe. "*Gevalt*! You're going to shoot your savior?" He motioned outside. Pure blue sky, wide plains, and expanse of green prairie grass rolling to the horizon. "Thought you might want some breakfast."

Thalia and I emerged from the wagon, stiff as if we'd slept in coffins. We stretched and crossed the grass to a little campsite where the Professor and Maximilian were cooking breakfast. Biscuits fresh from the pan, sizzling bacon, and an egg for the each of us—as close to a feast as one was likely to get out in the wilderness. We dined heartily.

They'd picked a little hill tipped with a creek for their rest. I went to the crest and peered out. A ways below, in the center of the eternal field, the town of Grasping Trunk waited. A few additions to its dusty streets. New structures birthed out of the loam for visiting homesteaders to enjoy, already as dusty as their ancient counterparts. New weathervane perched tall, catching the sunlight—a silver fish in a pond.

Otherwise, it looked the same now as it did when I was a boy.

I returned to the campfire. Professor Ashe sat there, mashing up some old apples for his pygmy mammoth. Further on, Maximilian and Thalia were playing fetch with Lady. The horse went straight down the hillside, leapt up to catch the thrown stick in the air, and galloped back without stopping.

Playing, like kids in the schoolyard. The way they ought to.

Ashe kept me watching. "She's a gem, your little one."

"Ain't exactly mine," I said. "I'm looking after her, I suppose."

"The same with Max," Ashe said. "His parents are in New York. Their tenement room's crowded enough without him, and with me he can at least earn some money and get a taste of the world." He shrugged. "Sometimes I wonder. I make him work, make him lie to earn his bread—feed him *treyf.*" He motioned to the pan, where a twist of bacon curled. "Maximilian Ashe isn't even his name. It's Motl Asch." He settled down on the bench. "I don't even know why I'm telling you this."

"Maybe I got a trustworthy face."

"I assure you, sir. You don't." He laughed dryly. "Perhaps it's good to unburden oneself."

Maybe I ought to give it a try. "Young Maximilian seems to hold you in high regard. And you're taking care of him—I can see that." Back on the hill, the boy started to race with Lady, stumbling his way over the hillside while Thalia shouted encouragement to both parties. "Thalia—I brought her back home to her grandparents. They despise her. And I'm going to deliver her to somewhere else, so she can end her quest without me. What sort of guardian is that?"

"So you say. And yet, you are by her side, taking care of her. I don't see you abandoning her anytime soon—so what else are you, if not her protector and champion?"

"You got a funny way of talking, professor."

"I'm as wise as King Solomon." He squinted down the hill. "I think someone's approaching."

Sure enough, a swirl of dust came racing along the little stitch-mark of a trail leading from Grasping Trunk and up toward us. Lord, I wished I had my buffalo rifle. "Thalia, Max!" I shouted up to them. "Get on up here!"

They kept playing. Ashe dashed down the hill, waving his fez and calling to them—that finally ended their game and got them up to the hill. I walked in front of them, my back to the fire, and let my vest fall to the ground—the better to reach the pair of pistols.

The dust cloud drew closer. A camel emerged with a fat man perched on the hump. He seemed to have the same sort of face as his mount, with pendulous lips and a bulbous nose marred with the redness brought on by an excess of a drink above a caterpillar moustache. Brown checkered trousers clashed boldly with his black waistcoat. He tugged at the reins and brought the camel to a complaining, grunting halt.

For a while, we stared at each other. Out here, in the wilds of the west, trusting a newcomer was akin to approaching a hornet's nest. And we didn't know if he was one of Mulberry's spies. Then Thalia gave him a curtsy. "Good morning, sir. I am Thalia Ridgeway. How do you do?"

Goddamn it! Her politeness had revealed us. Might as well admit the truth now. If he proved troublesome, I could always shoot him.

"I'm Corporal Clement Clarke. Who are you?"

He beamed. "Corporal Clarke, thank heavens." He swayed in the saddle. "Ned Buntline, sir. At your service." His eyes twinkled as Maximilian went to stand by his uncle. "Tell me, young miss and young sir, are you interested in dime novels? Popular amusements? Tales of the West? I create such marvels—each based in God's honest truth."

"Do you know *The High Plains Horror*?" Maximilian asked.

"Also known as *The Phantom Pachyderm of Prescott Peaks*?" Buntline finished. "One of my favorite yarns."

Thalia joined in. "What about *The She-Wolf's Wedding*, or, *Buffalo Bill and the Bandit Queen of the Dakota Dire Wolves*?"

"Wrote that one too. Under a *nom de plume*, of course."

This was getting on my nerves. "All right." I drew closer to the camel, who snorted and drew its head up—an angered serpent. "You got some skill with a pen. That's plain to see. Why are you here, Mr. Buntline?"

"Are you a friend of Wild Bill Hickok, Corporal Clarke? The protagonist of several of my frontier masterpieces?"

What was going on with Bill? "I am. What of it?"

"He's down in Grasping Trunk, ensconced in the Mammoth's Foot Saloon." He smoothed down his moustache. "Currently, he's under the guns of One-Eyed Ginny Wells and her gang. A most precarious situation." Ginny Wells—a bad penny. Just my rotten luck.

"Hell." I pointed to Ashe. "Saddle up the little mammoth. We're going into town."

He swallowed. "I fail to see how it's any business of mine, what…"

"Get moving or my irons will make it your business." I spat in the dirt and Professor Ashe hastened off, waving to young Max to help him. Thalia gave me a glare—a ferocious one. She didn't like me browbeating Professor Ashe. "Mr. Buntline, I thank you for the news. I'll go down and pull Wild Bill's fat from the flames."

"Excellent. I shall accompany you." He pulled up the reins of his camel. "It promises to be a brilliant piece of frontier theatre."

That it did—though the possibility of a concert of gunplay somewhat lessened the appeal. Apparently, Wells had gotten her old gang together, or acquired a new one. If they were anything like her in temperament, and if Wild Bill remained his usual self, it promised to be a lethal engagement. And yet, I could not fail to assist Wild Bill. He had my mammoth, for one reason.

And he was my friend.

We loaded up Professor Ashe's way and clambered aboard. This time, I took the coachman's seat beside the professor, while young Maximilian and Thalia settled into the back, opening the door so their feet could dangle over the road. Thalia held little Lady in her lap, and Goliath towed the whole crazy conveyance down the road to Grasping Trunk, with Buntline on his camel bringing up the rear.

Soon enough, we reached the town. It was strange, being home again after so long. There was the schoolhouse where I'd gotten my rump paddled. The same church loomed on the corner, where I'd fidgeted through many a long and tedious sermon. But plenty of new buildings had popped up, and fire and decay had taken down many that I remembered. They say that elephants never forget, and perhaps that is true, but man has them beat in that department. And memory's burden came down hard with every turn of the corner or passing porch. Made me think of how much I had changed, and that put a hollow in the bottom of my gut.

We reached the saloon called the Mammoth's Foot. My father had visited here now and then, though the old man was a teetotaler. He went to listen to speeches of prominent abolitionists, and for community meetings—the saloon was what passed for city hall back then. The single-story lump of bluebird-painted wood hadn't changed at all, apart from growing even dustier. Inside, raised voices. Outside, a half-score horses tied to the hitching post.

And General Butler waiting too, his ears flapping.

I sprang from the seat and hastened to the mammoth, who embraced me with his trunk. Then his eyes shifted, and a happy grunt left his mouth. Thalia had reached him, and his trunk encircled her too.

"You're all right!" She hugged him back. "You brilliant creature. Thank Heavens."

Harsh words came from inside. Doubtlessly, Wild Bill had entered to wet his whistle and that was where the trouble had occurred. At least it was just words—for now. I pulled the revolver from my coat and gave Butler's trunk a final pat.

"Clement Clarke!" A shout from a red-faced fellow huffing his way across the street. I squinted. The straw hat and necktie. The crimson cheeks. By God, it was Sheriff Campbell, who had done so little to protect Grasping Trunk over the years. Here he was, looking as befuddled as always. He stumbled to a halt, pausing to catch his breath. "Clarke—Clarke, you're back. After so long."

"That I am, sheriff." I pointed to the saloon. "Sounds like you got trouble."

"The Ginny Wells Gang. They come into town, now and then. Don't cause no trouble. Just let them drown their sorrows and they go on their way."

"Yeah, that sounds like you." I gave the pistol a spin. "Best stay out here."

"Clarke!" He swallowed. "Please. No shooting. If you can help it." Then a weak smile spilled across the tomato of his face. "And it's good to have you back in Grasping Trunk. After all these years."

Someone saying it was good to see me. Despite myself I smiled.

Then I entered the Mammoth's Foot.

Wild Bill was easy enough to spot. He stood with his back to the bar, a stuffed Smilodon head mounted above him—hard to tell who was the most ferocious. The bartender and piano man huddled behind the various engines of their trades, terrified of the violence which was soon to emerge. The rest of the saloon was occupied by five pistoleros covered in various degrees of dirt.

One-Eyed Ginny Wells was clearly their leader. She sat like some impudent devil on a throne, her boots on a table. She'd acquired her preferred weapon as well—a mean-old cut-down coach gun. It sat in a special holster on her belt, her fingers playing upon the two hammers.

Bill's eyes flicked to me. "Clarke! About time. Your mammoth's out front."

"I've seen him, Bill. Looks like you took good care of him."

"Ah, he was a peach." He spat on the floorboards. "Now, I find myself sharing drinks with a pack of scum. They've been talking big, thinking themselves the sovereigns of Kansas. I'm gonna topple their crowns."

"You just call the tune, Hickok!" Ginny Wells said. "And we'll start dancing."

I glanced at the doorway. Buntline stood there, a little pad and pen at the ready. Past him, Thalia watched in a state of worry. She had to be thinking what I was: even Wild Bill couldn't go against five guns and survive. Even with my help. And that Wells had helped us in the town of Jubilee and didn't deserve death.

"What exactly is the nature of your argument?" I asked.

One outlaw snorted and wiped his nose on his sleeve. He had a massive mud-colored beard, matching his hair, and looked as if no barber nor bath had ever touched his body. "They call me Dirty Dave." They called him true. "And I heard Wild Bill cut down John Wesley Hardin in Abilene. John Wesley Hardin's my wife's cousin. Or cousin's wife's brother, I forget—but he's kin, damn it, and he needs avenging." Dirty Dave's hand drifted low, brushing the revolver in a rawhide rig at his hip. Bill just watched and waited.

I doubted this man had kinship with John Wesley Hardin. More likely, he was drunk and spoiling for a fight—eager to be the man to kill a legend.

That was how real gunslingers acted. No battling each other for causes of love or justice or anything like that. It would be stupid disagreements, born of too much liquor, and the underlying need to see who was the tougher gunman. Male mammoths would lock tusks now and then—but never to the death. And never for such stupid reasons.

I sighed. "Bill, did you kill John Wesley Hardin?"

"That ain't the point…" He started.

"Did you?"

"No. We come close, but he never drew on me and neither did I on him."

I stepped between them. "You see? There's no call for this." I faced Wells, and forced all the good manners I could muster into my voice. "You saved us in Jubilee. I got no quarrel with you—I'll even let the bounty go." I waved to the window. "Thalia's outside. She likes you. Don't draw iron when she's around."

Wells stared at me for a long time. Sweat crept on my collar, and her remaining eye shone. Then she sighed deeply. "Why, Corporal Clarke, that's downright decent of you. Thalia Ridgeway's a good influence." She stood. "Boys, this old man ain't worth our time, nor our lead. Let's find a better watering hole."

The others stood—heeding her command. Except for Dirty Dave. He came to his feet, stepping in front of the saloon's only window—still keeping his hand by his six-gun. "You're getting soft, Wells. Getting talked down by some no-account bounty killer. Disgraceful. Maybe you oughtn't to run things. Maybe someone with sand ought to..."

I whistled. General Butler lashed out with his head, driving a tusk through the dusty glass of the window. His trunk slid in next. That length of fuzz could be gentle sometimes, but python-strong the next. It wrapped around Dirty Dave's shoulders and slammed him back into the wall, stopping him from drawing.

I moved in on him, but Wells reached him first. She smashed her sawed-off deep into his ribs. If Butler's trunk hadn't held him up, he would crumple. Then she delivered a rapid right hook to his face, grabbed his beard, and tugged until he wailed.

"You said something to me, Dirty Dave? You mention my name? All I heard was a donkey, braying away. That couldn't have been you—could it?"

Another whistle and Butler released Dirty Dave. He curled up and moaned on the ground.

"Grab him and let's go." Wells snapped her fingers and her assorted friends dragged Dirty Dave out the door. They departed, Wells hanging back a little. She faced me and touched the brim of her hat to me. "Reckon we'll see each other again, Clarke."

"Reckon so," I agreed, and followed her outside. Leaving Wild Bill to finish his drink.

The Ginny Wells Gang hopped onto their horses and galloped away. Dust rose in clouds as they crossed the main street of Grasping Trunk and vanished into the distance. Sheriff Campbell watched them go with a beneficent smile, while Buntline looked miserable. He didn't get his blood and thunder. Too bad for him. Young Maximilian, on the other hand, looked amazed that he had seen a dime novel come to life while his uncle surveyed the street. Thalia stood next to me and patted my arm. She was glad how I'd handled it.

Sheriff Campbell removed his frayed straw hat. "Thank you, Corporal Clarke. Thank you kindly. You saved us! Saved the…"

"Saved the undertaker from some fresh business." I pointed to the distance. "My folk's place. It still there?"

"Oh yes, sir. No one's moved in to the old Clarke Spread. Folks have offered, but I was always sure that they got turned down."

"That's a lie. Soil there's fit for producing nothing but rocks and hard times." But I was glad the farm remained. "Thalia, you and I will ride over there. We can spend the night, head north in the morning. Plan our next move."

"Very well." I knew what she wanted for that move, but she didn't bring it up here.

Professor Ashe massaged his chin. "A charming little town. Prosperous, I'm certain. Full of potential customers." He clapped his hands. "Max—open up the wagon. Bring out some bottles of Elohim Elixir and fetch your crutches. Be quick about it, *boychick*!" He doffed his fez to me. "I thank you, Corporal Clarke. You've brought me to some new customers."

"It wasn't my intention, but you're welcome." I pulled down the rope ladder and motioned for Thalia to climb up to the howdah. "So long."

"Farewell, Maximilian!" Thalia called.

The boy waved to her, his face reddening. "F-farewell, Miss Ridgeway. Thalia, I mean."

The batwing doors opened and Wild Bill emerged. He gave Buntline a glare and sent him running away, then held out his hand to me. "That was neatly done, Clem. I expected it to go differently. Me pulling my pistols, letting fly. Getting a good three or four of them outlaws before they got me—and that would be the end of my story. A good end. A bold end."

Did he want that to happen? Did he long for his blaze of glory? "I'm glad it didn't go that way."

"It just might." Wild Bill winked. "Story ain't over yet."

I clasped his hand, and then headed back to General Butler, thanking God and the stars above that I was not him.

We traveled to the west of Grasping Trunk. Soon enough, we left scrub country and the prairie behind and passed through a haze of trees. Autumn sunlight gleamed down and the branches cast dancing shadows over Butler's back and the howdah. The trail ended in a wide clearing, and there it was—the farm where I'd been born. Falling into disrepair now, the garden a victim of weedy conquest and the roof of our cabin pockmarked and broken. But it remained.

The memories came back. Buried bones, cast to the surface by rain and wind.

I let out a little sigh.

Thalia crawled closer. "Corporal Clarke, is this where you grew up?"

"Yes, ma'am." We rode closer to the ruined fence. "You see that branch there? Used to have an old swing dangling down. My pappy built it. He'd push me back and forth while reading bible verses." I waved to the field. "That's where Old Sam and I used to do the planting. He was a mastodon we got to pull the plow. I learned how to manage a mammoth on Old Sam. Just over there, by the creek."

She listened carefully.

We reached the fence and dismounted. General Butler ate his fill of the leaves from the numerous branches while I unpacked and led Thalia inside. The cabin's common room had a rusted stove, but I could get it working. Bedframes remained, and we could put down the bedrolls and sleep in those. While I took stock of our provisions, Thalia poked her head out the window.

"Oh, Corporal—you've got a garden!"

"My ma's." I joined her, looking at the weeds and wildflowers. "I was never much good at growing things."

"I'm certain that some seeds, water, and sunlight would work wonders out here." Thalia pushed open the door, the hinges complaining, and let Lady dash out to romp amongst the wilderness. She settled on the porch, the sunlight painting her shadow against the dusty floorboards. "Those stones there. Are those…"

"Tombstones. Yes, Miss Ridgeway. They are."

She clapped her hands and Lady ambled back. "I'm dreadfully sorry."

"You needn't be." I joined her on the porch. Once, we'd had a glider there and my pappy's old rocking chair, and he'd sit there and smoke his pipe while my mother and I sat on the cushions. She'd work her needlepoint and I'd count the stars. Just thinking about it turned my voice to a whisper. I'd never see them again. "My folks are down there. Reckon they'd be pleased to see some merry creature dancing above them."

Thalia listened, quietly.

I had to tell her—even if I didn't want to say it. "My father—my ma and I come home from a church meeting one day and found him hanging from that tree limb. Right next to my old swing. Border Ruffians were the ones who done it. We know, because they nailed a sign to his belly—He kills the Free Soil in Paradise—and left it for all to see. I dug the hole and laid him down. Day after, I mounted up Old Sam and rode off to join John Brown."

"You knew John Brown?"

"As bold a man as ever lived. As crazy a man as ever died." I shook my head. "Stayed with him and his riders for a while, but I weren't scarcely older than you, and so he sent me away before riding off to meet his destiny. Then, I just waited for the chance to get my vengeance, even as my hatred sickened my mother. Soon as the war started, I joined the Kansas Irregulars. Rode with them for a while, galloping about on Old Sam, and trading pistol shots with the like of William Clarke Quantrill and Bloody Bill Anderson—may those butchers burn forever in Hell."

"But your mother—she was still here?"

"I left her." Now, the hurting started. I left the porch and went to my ma's headstone. "Burning up with revenge, I left her to fear, and loneliness, and despair of losing all she had left. That killed her. I abandoned the Irregulars, got to see her on her deathbed, and buried her the next day. Then I rode off and joined the 2nd Dragoons."

Thalia joined me. She grasped my hand.

"I told her how much I loved her. How sorry I was for choosing to ride after hate and leaving her behind. But I don't know if she heard."

"She didn't have to," Thalia said. "She knew. I'm sure of it."

I closed my eyes. "Go on and start bringing supplies down from the General. Do what you can to ready dinner and I'll get some wood for the stove."

Being around her right then was more than I could bear. I stumbled away from the porch, heading for the trees. General Butler continued his grazing, stripping leaves from branch after branch and popping them into his constantly chewing mouth. After losing my mother, that mammoth was the friend I needed. That and the other drovers of the 2nd Elephantine Dragoons. Irish Johnny, and MacDougal, and Rufus Ridgeway too. They were my family when I had nothing left.

"Corporal!" Thalia called after me. I stopped. "They're proud of you. Your parents. I know they are."

I left her and went after my hatchet for the firewood.

After some work, we got the evening meal prepared. It weren't much, especially since Butler's saddlebags were getting mighty bare. We'd have to restock before traveling north, maybe in Grasping Trunk. The money from Thalia's grandparents would suffice to outfit us for the journey. Dinner consisted of the same fare we'd had for breakfast: biscuits, bacon, and beans. Thalia ate it without complaint, Lady curled up next to her on the floorboards as a fire danced in the stove.

I settled next to it, the warmth welcome. "We gotta talk."

"Indeed." Thalia crunched on a strip of bacon. "Shall we discuss your cooking skills? They need work, Corporal Clarke. They truly do."

"Not about that. About you—about where you're gonna go."

"You won't take me home again?"

"Nah—there's not much for you. Just grandparents that don't give a damn about you and assassins lying in wait." I opened the stove and gave one of the sticks a push, letting it tumble closer to the blaze. "Instead, I'll escort you north. I'll take you to Fort Fielding and Colonel Mortimer MacDougal."

"My father mentioned him. I believe he stayed in the Army, once the war ended."

"He certainly did. Your father mustered out and found your ma, I suppose, though they always wanted him back—which is what Mulberry was counting on. MacDougal and I stayed in Federal Blue. They sent us West." I stared at the blaze. "Fighting Indians. I lost my taste for it within a year. But MacDougal stayed on and even made colonel. He's running the Elephantry at Fort Fielding now."

"So I am to be deposited at his doorstep, then?"

"I'll introduce you, of course."

"And then ride away?"

"He's a full colonel, Thalia." I leaned back, settling on my bedroll. "He can help you far more than I can. He'll get his soldiers on it. Make sure Mulberry doesn't start no war with the Nations."

Thalia pouted. "I'd rather you stayed."

"I'd rather I ate tenderloin steak and washed it down with single malt scotch for every meal, but wishing don't make it so." I mopped up beans with my biscuits and scarfed them down. "I'm a bad influence on you."

"Not so. You have defended me ably. You saved my life at least three times." Her voice went higher, building to a crescendo. "And furthermore, consider your drinking. How many times have you drunken yourself into a stupor since you met me? How many times have you entered a gambling establishment and lost everything?"

"I've been too busy for any of that!"

She waved dismissively. "My point exactly. We are a fine partnership and it would be a shame to end it."

"Partnership." I set down my plate and stood. "I'll sleep outside, next to Butler. You can take my room, just over yonder."

Now, her voice rose—going temperamental and frustrated. "For God's sake, corporal, you are disgracing yourself!"

"What else is new?" I shouted back. Then I was outside. I joined General Butler, who lay on his side in a shaggy heap—already getting ready to snooze. I flapped out my bedroll and settled down next to him. "You believe that little harpy?" I plopped myself down, eager for shuteye.

General Butler farted, then. He released an utter torrent of wind, enough to make the grass shake and poison the air.

"Nobody asked you," I muttered and tried my best to sleep.

The next morning, we had a visitor at breakfast. The meal at least was a fine treat—eggs from the nest of a prairie chicken, which I'd found on the banks of the creek. A giant beaver had made the place his home in the absence of my family, and he floated there in the water and glared at me as I grabbed my treasure and hastened back to the cabin. That beaver was welcome to the land. By the time Thalia emerged, I had the eggs frying and served them alongside the last of our biscuits.

We were eating them on the porch when General Butler stirred and snorted. He had smelled something.

I had brought down the buffalo rifle from the howdah and I picked it up now. A man on horseback came down the trail to my farm at a trot. Prong? More of them Bracewell Detective goobers in their undertaker suits?

No. It was a man I recognized. A marshal—Bass Reeves.

I removed my hat and he did the same to his, revealing a dark face of beaten leather and a massive moustache. A cattleman's duster rested on his broad shoulders, not quite covering the Colt Double-Action at his hip. He dismounted and approached, morning sun dancing on his US Marshal's badge.

"Corporal Clarke." He took my hand in an iron grip. "How's the trail treating you?"

"Honestly, Marshal?" Reeves worked out of Fort Smith. Many were the unfortunate outlaws that I'd dragged back to him in exchange for a bounty. Reeves had no trouble going after lawbreakers himself, though. Matter of fact, I think he enjoyed the hunt greatly. "A mite poorly."

"I'm sorry to hear that." He touched the brim of his hat to Thalia, who had emerged. "Hello there, miss."

"How do you do, sir? I am Thalia Ridgeway."

"And I'm Bass Reeves, US Marshal." He didn't comment on the fact that I apparently had a child with me—I always gave Reeves my best, but we were far from chums. "Maybe you can help me, Corporal? I'm riding through Kansas, trying to bring an outlaw back to Fort Smith. Teach them the error of their ways."

"One-Eyed Ginny Wells, you mean?"

"No, though that is interesting that she's on the scout around here. I'm speaking of a bunko artist. A damn snake oil peddler calls himself Professor Alexander Ashe." None other than the fancy fellow with the wagon who had escorted Thalia and I west. "He sold plenty bottles over in Fort Smith."

"What were the results?"

"The hokum he sells, 'Elohim Elixir,' was supposed to be a restorative tonic. Regrow missing hair, turn a bald man's scalp into a mammoth's pelt. Except it didn't make hair grow. Instead, turned every tongue that tasted it bright blue, though. Including that of Judge Parker." The Hanging Judge. That didn't sound good. "He dispatched me personal to bring the professor back." His eye raised slightly. "You seen him?"

Lying to Marshal Reeves—there was nothing I wanted to do less. But Professor Ashe had helped me—at gunpoint—and I didn't want to put him in more hot water. Especially when he had a kid like young Maximilian depending on him. So I just stayed silent instead, and a very slow second passed.

Then Thalia decided the matter. "I'm afraid we haven't, sir." She smiled helpfully. "But if we do, and we contact you again, we'll be sure to let you know."

"You do that," he said. "Where you headed, then?"

"North, sir," Thalia explained. "Up through Nebraska, to Fort Fielding."

"Dangerous up there." Reeves returned to the back of his bay stallion. "I hear tell the Indian Nations are threatening war. And the blue-coat cavalry is eager to meet them. Might be the fighting we had a few years ago was just the rehearsal and the real war's coming." He shuddered. "I had my fair share of it. Hunting outlaws is the only fighting I want."

"Amen to that," I agreed.

He turned his horse around. "You take care of yourself, Clarke." Then he put some spur to his horse's flank and rode away.

I waited until the cloud of dust had faded and then glared at Thalia. "Lying to him. That was foolish—and you can bet he saw through it. Reeves is too smart to be played. Now he'll be at our back, seeking more."

"Nonsense. He's returning to the road, to seek Professor Ashe there." Then Thalia tapped her boot against the porch. "Oh—we need to go to Grasping Trunk immediately and warn him. Tell him to be on the lookout." She stepped in front of me. "Come now. Listen to your heart. Professor Ashe and Maximilian would be safely in St. Louis if it wasn't for us. At least you can do is warn him."

A stop in town. A quick warning. "We need to pick up supplies anyway. If we see him, we'll pass the warning along."

Thalia beamed. “I knew it. A heroic decision from the corporal.”

“Quit your caterwauling and mount up.” I clapped at General Butler, getting his attention. He had gone back to banqueting on the branches. “And you too, General. We’re burning daylight.” But there was a spring in Thalia’s step, and a flash of girlish joy in her eye. She’d won a battle, even if I didn’t want to admit it.

The two of us went back to Grasping Trunk, now unthreatened by the specter of a gun battle and bustling with midmorning traffic. Thalia and I rode General Butler over to the general store. As luck would have it, Professor Ashe stood outside, his wagon and pygmy mammoth behind him, and Maximilian making a show of going back and forth on a pair of crutches outside. He hardly noticed a mammoth arriving—an impossibility, to any but him—so fixed he was on hawking his bottles to passerby.

“My poor nephew, afflicted since birth with the cripple’s curse.” He waved to the kid, who had been examining the display of books in the store window. “And yet, a few drops of this restorative, refined with Kabbalistic secrets translated from the angels, and he can jig, reel, and waltz with aplomb.” He waved to a respectable-looking gent in a bowler hat. “You there—would you care to smell the substance yourself, before my nephew drinks it?”

I went over to him. “Howdy, professor.”

He spun around, speaking out of the corner of his mouth. “Your mammoth’s taking up attention. Taking it away from me.”

“Yeah. Sorry about that.” I gave Thalia a roll of bills. “Go in there and get some supplies. Big sack of corn for the General. If there’s anything leftover, you can get yourself a stick of peppermint or some other confection.” Then my eyes settled on Maximilian, who was staring in the same quiet awe at Thalia. “And he can go too. Pick himself out something.”

“Thank you, Corporal Clarke! Thank you.” He dashed inside in pursuit of candy—leaving his crutches behind. A miracle cure. Thalia followed, shaking her head, and just as eager for candy.

Ashe looked as if Butler had stomped on his foot. “You’re ruining my spiel.”

“This’ll ruin it worse. Marshal Reeves is after you. He’s nearby.”

He went pale. “*Gevalt*—I’m fixed.” He stumbled to the wagon, slamming the back shut. “If anyone wishes to purchase a bottle of Elohim Elixir, it will be on sale out the outskirts of town—within the hour.” His fez tumbled away and he struggled in the dust to retrieve it. “A misunderstanding with the good marshal. A mere misunderstanding.”

"If we see him, we'll pass the warning along."

"Go north," I suggested. "He's not likely to go that way."

"Thank you, Corporal Clarke. You are a mensch." He still held the bottle, and then a smile crossed his lips as he stared behind me. Looking at a potential customer, perhaps. "Excuse me, sir—would you care for a bottle?"

"No."

It was Orrin Prong's voice. Like the first rush of a blizzard's cold wind.

I turned. There was Prong, right there in the street. As bold as day. Normal folk were going back and forth, some farmer's wagon rattling across and sending squeaks from whining wheels up and down the town. They weren't to know, of course, but it was terrifying to see: everyone walking by normally while death himself stood there and faced me.

My hand drifted to the howdah pistol. "Mr. Prong. You don't got to do this. It's only money."

"Is that so?"

He took hold of his six-gun as the door opened and Thalia and Maximillian emerged, both talking excitedly as they worked on peppermint sticks and rock candy. The shopkeeper trailed after them, bearing our goods in a wheelbarrow. Thalia—right in his gun sights. His eyes flicked to her and we both knew what was going to happen.

I'd rather he drew and punched a hole through me. He was going to, though. But he'd hurt Thalia first.

Then Professor Ashe uncorked the bottle of Elohim Elixir and sent a rush of greenish liquid splashing out. The bottle sent its contents rushing out, painting Prong's chest in vibrant shades of emerald. He sputtered and tumbled back as the substance clung to his shirt and stained deeply.

That was what I needed. "Thalia—get on the mammoth!" I dashed past Prong first and punched him. My hand didn't shake. I could say that for myself, at least. My knuckles went into Prong's chin and he pitched back, falling into the dust.

Thalia followed, reaching the rope ladder leading to the howdah with Lady tucked under her arm. I picked her up and nearly tossed her onto General Butler's side. The terrified shopkeeper reached us next and I grabbed the pack of supplies and passed them up as well. No time to give the poor fellow a tip—even if I could afford it.

Then I got hold of the ladder and went up. General Butler was raring to go, stomping his hooves and waving his trunk in the air. One hand in front of the other, closer to the top. Was Prong back on his feet. Had he already drawn?

I got up and scrambled to the mahout's seat—then looked down.

Prong had drawn both revolvers—aiming straight at me. Pure murder in his eyes.

"Goliath!" Maximilian shouted to the pygmy mammoth, beckoning the little beast with both arms. He came charging from the wagon, snorting and shaking his trunk, wiggling his tusks, and struck Prong the way a lucky bull would take down a matador. Prong went crashing down to the earth, his shot ruined.

And we rode toward the edge of Grasping Trunk and made good our escape.

I kept watching, letting General Butler's sure tread and animal navigation guide our passage along the road. We'd just left a dangerous assassin in the company of a snake oil peddler and a boy. Thalia looked back too—terrified for her friends. Prong indeed made it back to his feet. He was shaking and weakened, but his trigger fingers were probably in fine condition.

He faced Ashe, already gesticulating and pleading out an apology. Would Prong shoot him down?

But then Sheriff Campbell arrived, along with the townsfolk. They surrounded Prong. Murder was acceptable to that demon. Getting caught red-handed for blowing away some innocent Hebrew on the street was not. I saw him facing them, glaring at their commentary—but no gunshots mingled with the gentle breeze on the prairie.

They were safe.

Thalia crept closer to me, Lady whinnying in her arms. "Corporal Clarke—that man. Prong. He's still on our trail."

"Evidently," I agreed. "But they'll keep him in town for a while. Campbell might make him spend the night in the jail cell before his masters can purchase his freedom. By then, we'll be in Fort Fielding."

"That's a relief."

And it was—but I felt another. From Wild Bill to the Ashes, my friends were safe. Thalia would be too. Soon as I was out of her life.

CHAPTER FIVE

CHILDREN OF THUNDER

We rode northward through the night. Thalia curled up in the howdah, wrapped in the buffalo robes that I kept in a little box on the back for that purpose as the chill increased. I slumbered too, catching an hour here or there as the sky darkened and the stars winked down from the black. I didn't mean to, but I was tired, and the gentle movement of Butler's gait transformed him into a humongous furry cradle set a-rocking by a kindly mother's hand. When bits of wakefulness stole upon my slumber, I'd look up at the vastness of the dark plains around me, the bits of moonlight catching the hint of frost in the air, and knew that we were safe in this land of wonderment.

So I was asleep when we went into the herd.

"Corporal Clarke." A gentle voice in my ear. I stumbled awake. Thalia motioned around us, keeping her voice to a whisper. "Look!"

General Butler had left the trail and wandered into the plains—and joined a herd of mammoths. Columbian Mammoths, the same species as him—though the occasional smaller mastodon had joined the pachyderm conclave. The great family was hard at work in grazing, their trunks reaching down and hauling up masses of prairie grass, still a-gleam with frost, that they popped into their mouths for regular, even rounds of chewing. Butler grazed alongside them, and his wild cousins accepted him without qualms.

Thalia opened her mouth, but I put a finger to my lips. She heeded the message, and merely crawled around the howdah for a better look at the numerous elephants.

This was a decently sized herd—perhaps a score of adults and that number again in juveniles and calves. The matriarch, a massive beast with saber-tooth scars etched white against the brown of her fur, stomped ahead of us toward a slight hill, staring at a copse of trees in the distance. A pair of younger males, not yet old enough to go off on their own or reach the General's advanced state of wisdom, gave their tusks a little action in a friendly tussle. The babes of the herd, an adorable pack, traipsed around General Butler, and he gave them a warning, whining trumpet as they played.

Thalia crept back to me, keeping her voice to a whisper. "It's—it's profound. They are miracles."

"You should've seen these plains a decade ago," I said. "There were herds that dwarfed this bunch. You'd see them stretched to the horizon, longhorn bison and the occasional grazing sloth with them too."

"Hunted, I suppose."

I patted Butler's knobby head. "Or domesticated. But yeah, hunters went to work. Mammoths are not as easy prey as buffalo, but ivory and mammoth hide are worth plenty. And then there's folks just looking for a thrill."

The matriarch mammoth let out a sudden snort. She hoisted her head in the air and trumpeted, a brassy reverberating note that carried across the whole herd. A watchman's clarion. A second later, a gunshot thundered—a terrible, clear boom. It blazed through the dawn. Didn't strike a mammoth, but not for lack of trying.

"Goddamn it!" I tightened knees. "Thalia—put a rope around your waist and hold tight." I shifted, making Butler go to the right—trying to match the herd.

Already, they were starting to panic. The other mammoths followed the matriarch's trumpets, the cows forming a protective circle around the calves while the young bulls galloped as outriders along the flank. One bull came rushing toward the General, and I shouted and urged my mount on. He pounded his way past, the younger male sliding behind him, and went at the same speed as the herd.

A charge—a stampede. They crashed their way across the prairie, dust and grass flying from heavy footfalls. When those cowboys moved their cattle north, it had to be like this, but no cow was ever the size of a mammoth. I pulled up my bandanna for the dust. Behind me, Thalia crouched low, gripping a rung on the howdah while Lady whickered and kicked her legs. She slipped free, and I lunged back and grabbed the horse by a tiny leg. She dangled low, terrified, until I swung her back into Thalia's arms.

We neared a collection of dusty, dingy hills, right on our flank. I peered ahead, trying to see through the dust. Yeah—a group of men there, emerging from the tall grass. Probably horses and wagons behind them, to haul back the ivory and mammoth head trophies from the kill. They'd put a rifleman in the trees to fire and scatter the herd, driving them closer to the guns of the hunters on the hill. These boys would unleash a torrent of fire from their elephant guns, and probably bag something big.

Somewhere in the fear and panic, anger rose. These wild mammoths weren't hurting no one. I'd known from my time with Old Sam and General Butler that the species wasn't composed of brutes—they were loyal, and kind, and wished to love and be loved in turn. And here were a couple of trophy hunters, eager for mammoth heads on their walls and ivory to top their walking sticks, about to unload on them with express rifles.

I twisted General Butler to the side, sending him through the herd. "Corporal!" Thalia cried as a she-mammoth, sheltering a trio of little ones, surged closer. They were between us and the hills and the hunters.

"Come on, Butler!" I gripped his head close. "You are the soul of energy! You are speed incarnate!"

He put on a burst of speed and raced ahead, stepping right over a little mammoth. I caught a glimpse of the small creature, staring in amazement at the bigger Columbian towering over him, and then we were past the female, her tusks nearly grazing Butler's rump, and heading straight for the hill.

And the guns.

I went tall in the mahout's seat, waving my arms. "Don't shoot! People here! Don't shoot!"

One express rifle blazed—the boom rushing over heads, and then we galloped closer and I caught a look at the shooter.

He stood in the grass, a tall fellow in a Norfolk jacket and bowler—more dressed for blasting grouse than elephants. From my height, I could make a neat cowcatcher beard and even—oh yes—a monocle wedged in his right eye. He still had his elephant gun raised, pointed straight at Butler.

"Drop your weapon, your lordship! That elephant's got riders!" A tall fellow grabbed his gun and shoved it down. I recognized that man. A fringed jacket and scarlet neckerchief, hay-colored hair worn long and slick with tonic, and a familiar brightness to his eyes. It was William Cody—Buffalo Bill. Now, he pushed the express rifle down and waved madly to the others. "Ceasefire, boys! Ceasefire! We're here to bag wild mammoth—nothing else."

"Corporal." Thalia called to me. "You'd better slow General Butler or he might stomp someone."

I had half-a-mind to do some stomping. But I worked my knees back and brought him to a canter, and then a trot, and then reached the hill and stopped.

Mr. Norfolk sprang up, arms flailing. "Dreadfully sorry, old boy. Dreadfully sorry. Simply didn't see you there riding with the wild elephants. We must thank providence that a dreadful accident did not befall you or your daughter." He beamed to Buffalo Bill. "Providence and our guide, Mr. Cody."

"I told your lordship a thousand times—you don't work that trigger until I tell you." Cody sighed. "I'm sorry." Then he squinted. "Clement Clarke, is that you?"

"That's right." I nodded to Thalia. "And I'm looking after this little one."

"Is that a fact? I heard you weren't with the Dragoons no more." That's where I had last seen Cody—we had met in Kansas before the war, and later he scouted for us Elephantry boys and hunted buffalo to fill our bellies. "But I thought you wouldn't be so stupid to go riding with a herd of wild mammoths."

"I'm doing all sorts of stupid things lately."

"True enough." He pointed back over the hill. "Why don't you follow us to camp? We can get you some breakfast. Least we can do, after shooting at you."

The Norfolk Suit craned his neck, watching the mammoths. "What about my trophy?"

"Keep your trousers on, Lord Spoone." Cody shook his head. "They ain't extinct yet."

But with men like Lord Spoone plugging away at them and Buffalo Bill guiding the hunting expeditions, I wasn't sure how long that would last.

Cody brought us down the hills and to a true oddity: a little bit of European fanciness, transported into the West. This Lord Spoone traveled in style. He had a small army of wagons set behind him, with white tents in neat rows containing a study, kitchen, and dining room right there on the prairie. Servants hastened back and forth to prepare his breakfast—steaming buffalo liver and fried quail eggs, served with coffee and tea in silver cups. He even had napkins.

He was nice enough to share that breakfast with Thalia and me, and for a squad of grooms to take care of General Butler. After taking a shot at us, it was the least he could do. General Butler swiped the cap of one groom and sent it whistling away, until I slapped his flank and made him behave. Then we settled down at the table and dined.

Thalia had good table manners, sawing neatly at the grub and carefully mixing sugar into her tea. "So, your lordship, what brings you to the west?"

"Hunting, my dear child. The thrill of the hunt." Lord Spoone had changed into a velvet smoking jacket with a monogram on the breast pocket. "I have sought game on three continents and nothing compares to the American West. The tiger of India, the cape buffalo—they are mere appetizers compared to the glorious meals of America's beasts." He gave a brotherly smile to Cody. "I heard of Mr. Cody's good work with the Grand Duke Alexis of Russia and knew that I could hire none other to be my tutor to the ways of the American wilderness."

"You enjoying yourself doing that, Cody?" I asked Buffalo Bill. "Being his tutor to the ways of the American wilderness?"

Cody rolled his eyes. "What are you doing out here, Clarke?"

"Going to Fort Fielding. This little one's lost her father. I'm taking her to Colonel MacDougal—you remember him—and to safety."

A dark look appeared in Cody's keen blue eyes. "Little safety to be found up north, friend. I don't know if you've heard, but tensions are rising between the white man and the Indian Nations. Might be time for the war path yet again."

"That's precisely what we mean to stop, sir," Thalia said.

"A noble cause, my dear, but you must not proceed northward." Lord Spoone raised his finger—making his grand proclamation. "It is far too dangerous for a child."

"I've told her that," I said. "She won't be swayed."

"He's right." Thalia smiled slyly as she cupped some sugar cubes for Lady.

"At least we can offer you some supplies." Cody stood and drank the last of his coffee. "Come on, Corporal. Let me show you what we have."

He led me away from the table. Thalia and Lord Spoone could chat some more about clotted cream or pocket squares or whatever it was fancy folk discussed. I followed him away from the dining room and to another, which served as a sort of pantry and armory. I peered through the sacks. Hardtack and bullets would be useful up north.

Cody hooked his thumbs in his belt. "What are you doing, Clarke?"

"Taking Miss Ridgeway to the Fort Fielding. Like I said."

"I mean in general. You still bounty hunting? Drinking? Gambling?" He sighed. "That'll put you in an early grave."

"At least I'm not like James Butler Hickock—the other Bill."

That perked him up. "How's he doing? I ain't seen Wild Bill since our theatre show went bust."

"He's taking risk after risk." I sounded scared, and maybe I was. "I caught him trying to start a gunfight with the Ginny Wells Gang—a gunfight he had more than a good chance of losing." It hurt to say. Wild Bill was our friend. "I think he wants to die. It doesn't make much sense."

"Yes, it does." Cody stared into the distance. "Folks like me and you and Wild Bill—we are creatures of the West. And the West is finishing up." He pointed to the corral, where General Butler loomed giant amongst the horses and camels. "Many believe that the mammoths and other great creatures should have gone extinct centuries ago—that they are living fossils, who only capricious fate has spared from demise. Well, fate has turned against them. Their time is up. Now, like the mammoth, we gotta change."

"That's what you're doing? Playing nursemaid to Lord Fancy Pants?"

"I am portraying the legend." He patted his buckskin jacket. "You should see the crowds we got for our performances back east. Even if the scripts were Buntline's nonsense and my acting is akin to that of a sloth, everyone wants to see it. They all want a taste of the West. That is the way I'll survive. Wild Bill, it seems has not found his means of survival. But what about you?"

"Me?" I asked. "I don't know..."

"You want my advice? I'll give it, free of charge." He pointed to the table. "That girl. I saw the fear you had on mammoth-back. You care for her. More than you cared for anything during your time as a soldier or a bounty hunter. Perhaps you consider yourself her savior. No, Clarke. She is yours." He clapped his hand on my shoulder. "Take what you need. His Lordship brought plenty. I'll see your mammoth fed and then you'd better get going. You've a long way to travel."

He left me with the beans and bread. I gathered what I could, tucked the rucksack over my shoulder, and started back to the corral. The girl, my savior. What a load of mammoth dung! I was doing just fine before I met her.

Then the alley in the French Quarter stained with my vomit came blasting back. That and my gambling habits. I looked back at the tented dining room, where Thalia was charming Lord Spoone. She was treating him with kindness. The way she did everyone.

Another turn brought me to a tent opposite the corral. Cold sunlight glinted on something—a glint I knew. I peeled back the flap and looked inside.

Mammoth ivory. Three pairs of tusks, all of various sizes. One from a Columbian, one from an Alaskan Woolly that must have made its way down from Canada and into his gunsights, and another from a mastodon. That mastodon's head lay on a sort of sawhorse. Apparently, His Lordship traveled with a taxidermist. He'd carved up the mastodon, scooping out the brains and replacing the eyes with dead marbles. They stared at a similarly mangled head of a giant sloth, a Longhorn Bison, and even a big capybara.

I looked at those remains. They put the spark to the tinder in my heart.

Footsteps on the dry grass behind me. "Impressive collection, eh?" Lord Spoone asked. "I find them even more impressive than the elephants I've bagged on safari. I'm thinking of putting them in my countryside estate. If you're ever in Surrey, you'll have to…" He trailed off. The look in my eyes must have told him that continuing was foolish.

"You get a thrill out of it?" I asked. "When the calves wail for their murdered mothers? You like that sound?"

He swallowed. "My good man—I am—I am a sportsman."

I gripped his necktie and tugged him close. "They fear. They love. They mourn. You kill them and you call it sporting?"

"Clarke!" Thalia shouted. She ran to me, Lady galloping next to her. Cody followed, a glare in his eye. "Corporal—please." She was next to me, frightened—of me and what I was fixing to do. "He doesn't mean any harm."

I let go.

"You'd best leave now, Clarke," Cody said.

I took a final look in the tent flap. "Reckon so." Then I started for the corral, where General Butler waited. He knew I was upset and gave me a nuzzle with his trunk as I went up on his back. Thalia clambered up next and then we set off. Leaving Cody to his guiding of Lord Spoone and all the fine game they'd hunt.

It wasn't worth it, being angry at Spoone. He was just one fancy fellow, wanting to get some ivory for his mansion. Legions of hunters had already picked the plains nearly clean, cutting down mammoths wherever they could be found. The surviving herds made their way cautiously across the land or stayed north, in the Nations, where the whites had not yet conquered. It was like Cody had said: the West was reaching its end, and soon would exist only in old pictures and stories.

And men like him, or Wild Bill, and me had to keep on living in what was left.

We didn't see more mammoth herds as we rode north, now sticking mostly to the roads. Some wild camels sipping at a watering hole—then perking up and galloping into the distance, pursued by a tawny, long-tailed blur that had to be a cheetah, and a few mastodons stripping lone trees for leaves. The weather worsened too. Cold, the likes of which an easterner cannot fathom, seeped into the air as dark clouds billowed overhead. I had some old quilts in the saddlebags and I wrapped Thalia up before doing the same to me.

She looked into the distance with my spyglass, wind stirring her hair. "I don't see Fort Fielding. Will we reach it soon?"

"Nah. Got a friend's cabin nearby. He knew your father—another Dragoon. Hoping we can spend the night."

"Oh." She hesitated. "How long until we get there?"

I let out a little chuckle. "You know, I'd ask my parents the same question during our every journey. Whether it was riding in the wagon to town or taking a big trip to look at some horses for sale in Missouri—when are we gonna get there?"

She wasn't amused. "Well, when?"

"Long enough."

Then, another noise crept out over the darkness and the wind. A cold sort of scream, which made Butler trumpet and sent a chill dancing down my neck. A howl, high and long and then echoed by a score of others. A whole chorus, cutting through the dark.

"Let me have that spyglass." I accepted it from Thalia and squirmed around in the saddle. Peering back at the tall grass.

Sure enough, wolf eyes glowed white in the fading light. Great brindle, red, and black forms, moving through the prairie grass. Not Timberwolves nor gray wolves but Dire Wolves—the biggest and meanest variety out there. A big Columbian mammoth like Butler might not be easy prey—but he was alone and that made him weak.

Thalia crept closer to me on the howdah. "Wolves." Spoken quietly.

"I see them." I gave Butler's head a pat, stirring him from a walk to a more purposeful trot. "Wolves—even the Dire variety—aren't unusually inclined to go after people. Or the animals they're riding. Unless they're hungry." And human hunters have already picked the prairie clean. With winter coming fast, they must be desperate enough to take us on. I reached back, taking up the buffalo gun and letting it rest on my knees. "We need to find someplace to stop."

"Stop?"

"Put our backs to something, so they can't get around us. Maybe get a fire going. Wolves aren't fond of fire."

Up above, thunder rolled. God clearing his throat. The boom echoed over the prairie and the rain started coming, streaking in silvery lines that danced in the growing wind. I swore bad enough to make Thalia wince. Rain—that would make the fire difficult. The wolves would like it just fine. They could sneak around us in the downpour and the wind, hiding in the darkness before they struck. Would they try and take Butler? Nah—but they'd chew up his legs until Thalia or I dropped, and then grab us and drag us away. Wolves didn't mind if their meals were soggy.

"How about over there?" Thalia pointed to an outcropping, a jagged spur of land emerging from the plains. It had a mass of pretty prairie wildflowers, all gentle blues and golds, sprouting from the top. Not quite big enough to be a hill, but it had some rise to it, and the wolves wouldn't get around. "Would that work?"

"Bless your keen eyes, Miss Ridgeway." I directed Butler toward the hillock. "Come on now. Almost there."

General Butler brought us to the rise soon enough and I sent down the ladder. Thalia and I descended, a bundle of firewood under her arm. She plopped it down in the shelter made by the curl of the hill, and went to work with flint and tinder. Lady curled up next to her, rain plastering her little mane to her neck, and whinnied piteously. I had my rifle and General Butler standing tall next to me—but I didn't feel safe.

The rain was coming down real bad now. It drummed against the brim of my hat and sliced under my collar, trickling cold down my spine. It plastered Butler's light, bristly fur to his flanks and ran off his tusks. I put the buffalo rifle to my hips and watched the tall grass ahead of us. Glowing eyes—the Dire Wolves, fixing us in place.

They came from the side, making a rush. A pair of orange-pelted giants, fur matted by the rain and teeth flashing. Their jaws just about the height of my belly button. I fired at one, the muzzle flash blinding and sending him dashing away. The other went past me—going for Thalia and Lady.

The smallest targets.

General Butler lashed out, matching his blow with a trumpet. He caught the wolf with a kick. The blow sent the huge canine hurtling back, its whine shattered as it crashed into the prairie. I couldn't help smiling—it's good to have a Columbian Mammoth watching your back. But the smile vanished as Butler's trumpet switched to one of pain.

Two more wolves had attacked him from the flank. A tawny beast settled on his foot, biting deep. The other went for Butler's underside—trying to get some fangs into his guts. No time to put another round in the rifle. I charged in instead. Butler hefted a foot in panic, nearly giving me a kick, and I ducked under it. The wolf was leaping up, not noticing me. I swung the rifle around, the butt connecting right with his jaw.

Another growl, but he dashed away, brushy tail wiggling as he escaped.

The other wolf let go of Butler's leg and decided I was easier prey. It struck me—a red-furred artillery shell. The skull banged deep into my gut, my legs lost purchase, and I tumbled down. Those jaws were snapping as I took hold of its neck. Going for my throat. Or at least my face. My legs kicked out. It growled and I wailed.

Thalia raced to help. "Let go of him! Away with you!" She had a chunk of firewood, barely ablaze, and bashed that against the wolf's back with all her vigor. Sparks flew from the makeshift club. But the wolf wouldn't let go. A tooth scraped my chin. No more than an errant razor, but the next bite might find firmer purchase.

A rifle shot thundered. The wolf dropped on me. Hot blood stained my face. Then it lay still—solid weight on my ribs, enough to crush my heart.

More gunshots. Trumpeting from other mammoths. Shouts mingled with the thunder and then panicked howls as the dire wolves made their retreat. Even hunger wouldn't make them fight a losing battle.

I looked to the side. Three mammoths had come out of the storm—a pair of mastodon bulls and a bigger Columbian cow. All had riders. A flash of lightning came down, casting brilliant light over the three. Their howdahs had been constructed of wood, the bones of sloth and buffalo, and held in place with leather strips. Spears and quivers of arrows, beaded scabbards for rifles resting neatly in place. Decorations on the sides of the beasts too. Handprints etched in white and red, masses of stripes. Telling stories of past victories and past kills.

All Indian mammoths.

Reminded me of the Indian name for the pachyderms—Children of Iya, the Storm-Father, brother of Iktomi the Spider-Trickster. He roared and crashed his way over the earth, trampling everything in his path. The mammoths were his progeny. Children of Iya. Children of Thunder.

They drew closer. I sat up, touching my chin. Blood pooled around my fingers. A rope ladder descended from the big Columbian and an Indian descended. Cheyenne, Lakota, or Blackfoot—I couldn't tell. A woman, though. She wore a dark fringed jacket, a single hawk feather in her long hair, and a Winchester repeater rested on her shoulder. Other warriors descended, and more waited on the backs of the pachyderms.

Maybe the wolves were preferable.

I reached to my vest. The revolver. My arm ached, but I still gripped it.

Thalia swallowed and came to her feet. She faced this Indian she-devil—

and curtsied. "Thank you. I am so very grateful. I believe you saved his life." She must be trying to keep her composure. "My name is Thalia Ridgeway and this is Corporal Clement Clarke, my guardian. How do you do?" Spoken as if she was in a drawing room, not a rain-strewn prairie.

The Native warriors stared at each other, saying nothing. The woman—their leader, perhaps—called something in her language to the others. One lean fellow with braids over his shoulder let out a sudden laugh.

What were they planning to do?

Then another voice came from the mammoth. "Pleased to meet you, Miss Ridgeway. How do you do?" A scrawny figure nimbly descended the rope ladder and joined us, giving a wave. "Carlos Montezuma. At your service." He bowed.

A boy. Perhaps in his early teenage years, with a tallness still a stranger to his body. He wore a pale, duck white suit and a little bowtie, a broad-brimmed hat shading short hair from the rain, which he removed in a sweeping, gentlemanly gesture that left him sodden. It was bizarre. What was this child doing with the war party? And with a name like Carlos Montezuma?

The woman switched to English. "You're holding close to a pistol, Corporal Clarke. Take my advice—let it go."

"You ain't working hard enough to convince me."

"I assure you, sir, that's as polite as Running Eagle can be." Montezuma walked between us. "But I promise you—no harm shall come to you or Miss Ridgeway." He glanced back at Running Eagle and uttered something in her language—the words clumsy. He repeated it in English. "Please—the truce. We must remember the truce." He gave her a nervous smile. "If it is to be broken, let the *wasichu* break it."

"I doubt we'll have to wait long." She slung the rifle over her shoulder. "What were you doing out here, besides getting eaten by wolves?"

I forced my hand free off the revolver. Stood slowly, and next to Thalia. "Traveling."

"Where to?" Montezuma asked brightly.

I had to give them something. "A friend's house..."

"Irish Johnny?" Running Eagle asked. "Only house near here."

"You know him?"

"He's all right."

Montezuma grinned. "High praise for a white man from Running Eagle. Not that I blame her, of course." He walked closer to us and offered his arm to Thalia. "We would be honored to escort you to the home of Irish Johnny. If you would be so good to as to allow us." He spoke politely, but a look at Running Eagle told me that we didn't have a choice.

"Carlos Montezuma. At your service."

He led her back to General Butler, who had intertwined his trunk with the Columbian cow. They were getting along splendidly. It was more than I could say for us humans.

The storm lessened, giving way to a cool, clear prairie night. Our odd procession crossed the plains, starlight twinkling above through fading storm clouds. The rain had lessened from a cruel, raging downpour to a glistening drizzle now tinged with flecks of frost. It wasn't particularly comfortable, but at least it was an improvement. And it suited Thalia and the young Carlos Montezuma—or Monty, as he wished to be called—who chatted amiably as our mammoths rode side by side.

"A product of the sideshow, the medicine show, and the theatre. That's me." Monty gave his hat a flap, dispensing of rainwater. "Pima Indians raided my village—Apache—when I was but a babe in arms and stole me away. Later, an enterprising Italian purchased me for a few dollars and a pair of camels."

"You were—purchased?" Thalia asked.

"Oh yes." He spread his fingers, envisioning a marquee. "I was christened Carlos Montezuma, and played the part of Azteka, the Apache prince of Cochise, in a few theatrical productions. Ned Buntline penned them and Buffalo Bill played the starring role."

"We've met both of them. Quite recently."

"Is that so? And how are old Ned and Mr. Cody?"

I cut in. "Monty—how'd you go from playing Indian on the stage to riding with real ones out here?"

His gaze darkened. "Real ones?" I swallowed. "No, no—I suppose it's not your fault. An Indian's not an Indian unless they're riding on a mammoth and sporting a war bonnet. Isn't that so?" He sighed. "I'm a college student. University of Illinois. They admitted me, despite my age." He smiled proudly. "I'm going to be a doctor."

"Cured my piles," Running Eagle called.

"But I cut my education short. I'm not descended from any of the so-called Indian Nations, but the war may start here and I must play the part of peacekeeper."

Thalia beamed. "That's so—so noble."

"I just don't want any more unnecessary bloodshed. Not like what happened to my people, back home." Now, the confidence left him. He was a boy again—an orphan and one trying desperately to play the part of a man. "I'm trying to prevent it. Any way I can."

"How's that working?" I asked. "Playing peacemaker?"

Running Eagle muttered something in her language. "Your people aren't doing much to make it easy." That sounded plenty truthful to me, but it still hurt to hear. After all, I'd served my time as an Indian Fighter. I knew how truthful her words were—proven right by the simple fact that all this, the entire continent, had once been their land. "Right now, it's Sitting Bull against Crazy Horse."

"Do you know them?" Thalia asked young Monty. "The Great War Chiefs?"

"I am a mere child next to such great men," Monty replied—belying the fact that he was a child. "It is exactly like Running Eagle says. Sitting Bull advocates peace and caution. He believes that the Nations will not survive another war. Better to gather strength, breed our mammoths, get weaponry from the *Syndicat Metis*, and wait. But Crazy Horse…" He sighed. "There is little dissuading him from conflict. He saw the Little Bigtusk and wants an encore."

The Little Bigtusk. Their most shocking victory of all. "But which one will win?" I asked.

"Peace—I hope." But he didn't sound so sure.

"Up ahead—there is the home of your friend." Running Eagle stood in the howdah, balancing expertly on the shifting platform. She gestured to a hill piercing the prairie—an island in the sea of dancing grass. It had a little farmhouse, with sheep and goats spread along the hillside in furry, slumbering clumps, watched over by a trio of watchful guard llamas. "Go and visit them. And leave us."

"How do you plan to do it?" I asked Monty. "Get peace?"

"I shall head a party of diplomatic envoys," he exclaimed. "A peace delegation. We'll demand respect for the borders—keeping the Black Hills safe. Once that's clarified, I trust that your cavalry and the settlers will keep to their word and we'll have no more trouble."

A smirk from Running Eagle.

"Let's hope your delegation succeeds, son," I said. "I've seen mammoth war. When us white men did it and a little of when our folk battled it out. It ain't pretty."

"I'll take your word for it." He shuddered. "Farewell, Corporal Clarke. Farewell, Miss Ridgeway."

"So long!" She called to him, giving Monty a wave—and her face had reddened. I suppose schoolboys weren't the only ones who could be smitten. And I didn't mind it much. Getting smitten was what kids did, occasionally. So it was a trace of normalcy for Thalia, and I was glad she got to have it.

Monty magnanimously waved back and the Indian mammoths stomped away, giving a parting trumpet which General Butler politely returned. They trudged away, moving at a good trot, and headed into the distance. Up above, the moon had emerged from the clouds and cast silver along the falling frost and streaks of rain, making the great beasts look like jewels rolling along black velvet.

I looked back at Thalia. "We'll be there soon and then y'all can rest. You let me do the talking." I had General Butler switch to a canter, his heavy feet casting up half-frozen muck as we neared the farm. "God—another war. Mulberry doesn't have to work hard to set it off, that's for certain."

"You want it stopped?" Thalia asked.

"Damn right I do. Another war—and you know Sitting Bull's right. Elephantry gives his people an edge, but it ain't much of one compared to the might of the United States Army. It'll be a costly war, but the Indians would be crushed. And then folk like Spoone will come in, shooting and killing and taking every chunk of ivory they can get.'

"I agree. It must be stopped." She took hold of my arm. "We can stave off war, corporal. Make this fight yours. Then, victory is guaranteed."

She had gotten me going. I shrugged off her arm. "Pipe down. Stay warm. We'll be out of the cold soon enough." I left it at that. Thalia drew away, wrapped her and Lady in the quilt, and pouted. I left her to her sulking.

Soon enough, we reached Irish Johnny's farm. I led General Butler up the rise and to the hill. We stirred up a few sheep, goats, and the guard llamas let out their calls, waking up everyone. I wasn't too worried about waking up Irish Johnny. He always kept late hours and it was still before midnight. Sure enough, when we topped the hill, Johnny was sitting on the porch with a double-barreled shotgun across his knees, working on a hand-rolled cigarette.

He stood up, setting the shotgun aside. "Clarke." Only a flick of a smile on his hairless lips as he beckoned us down in his pure brogue. Overalls and a mackinaw formed his uniform, though he still wore his old Union kepi. I might have just returned from a stint of reconnaissance out in the swamps for all the feeling in his greeting.

"Johnny." I kicked down the rope ladder and descended. He crossed the porch and we clasped hands. "Quite a spread you got."

"The result of hard work and canny business sense, corporal." He stared back—looking up at Thalia. "You'll be wanting dinner, then?"

"If you wouldn't mind. Place to sleep as well. For me and the girl." I leaned closer. "It's Rufus's daughter."

"How do you do?" Thalia asked. "I am Thalia Ridgeway."

He nodded curtly. "You'll stay, then, as long as you want, and eat the finest food I have in my larder." Johnny walked up to the porch. "You'll have the pick of my wares as well, and I'll no take no payment in kind. No arguments now." He wagged a finger at as me as he held the door for us.

That was like Rufus. The legacy of his friendship had been writ in fire upon all our lives.

Irish Johnny's home had the lived-in look of a place that was cleaned only on occasion and with reluctance. Still, his kitchen was well-stocked and he set us down at a little table that got the warmth of the stove and commenced to warming up and slicing some bread. He served that with goat cheese, fresh from his stock, and then some fruit tarts for dessert, slick with icing and delicious.

Poor Thalia ate, but was swaying in her seat. She needed rest—I did too.

Johnny could see it. "Miss Ridgeway, you'll take the guest room. Clarke—the Chesterfield's comfortable enough. I've got plenty of blankets. You go and rest and I'll see Butler to the barn. Plenty of hay for him to enjoy." Johnny then started down the corridor. "Let me bring out the merchandise. I owe you that. I owe all of you."

As his footsteps faded away, Thalia stared at me. "He seems devoted to you."

"To your father too. And to MacDougal." I paused. "I suppose it's on account of we kept his secret."

Her eyes widened. "Secret?"

Irish Johnny returned, hefting a massive crate with something pillar-shaped poking out the top. "Irish Johnny—that's the nickname they gave me. But the name—the false name—could've been Irish Janey." A little smile crossed his lips as he set down the crate. "That's the beauty of America. Of the West. You can be what you truly are." A cloth covered the crate and he whipped it off with a magician's flourish. "You just have to be ready for trouble."

It was a Gatling gun. Well, not the whole weapon. The big wheels weren't attached, it didn't have the case of ammunition, and it was smaller too.

Still, Irish Johnny might have just dropped a rattlesnake on the table. "Damnit!" I nearly choked on my fruit tart. "Where'd you get that?"

"Fort Fielding. I have some old military contacts. A boy-o here and there who doesn't mind if a piece of equipment goes missing, in exchange for a cut of the profits." Cut of the profits? "I thought you knew, Clarke—I ain't only raising sheep and goats out here."

He was an arms dealer. "Who are you favorite customers?"

"Indians. Outlaws. Whoever pays." He patted the Gatling. "But for Rufus, you'll get this *gratis*. She's a special little number—designed to be mounted and fired from the back of a howdah."

"That's—that's not why we're here, Mr. Johnny." Thalia cleared her throat. "We merely wish to spend the night. Before going to Fort Fielding."

"So you *don't* want the Gatling gun?"

"Appreciate the gesture, friend," I said. "But no."

He looked almost disappointed. "All right. Get some rest. And tomorrow, you tell me what's going on." He returned the cloth to its position above the gun. "But I'll tell you this, Clarke—if that girl is Rufus's daughter, and you're looking after her instead of him, it means he's gone. And if you're all the way out here, it means you're running from something. So he didn't go peacefully. We'll be wanting revenge, then, and I've got the weapons to get it."

Except it wouldn't be vengeance against some owlhoot with a pistol, but with Mulberry and his vast conglomeration of power. The Bracewell Detective Agency and Orrin Prong. Just thinking about him gave me the willies.

I drank the cup of sheep's milk and stood. "Good night, Johnny."

Thalia and I split up and we bedded down. A hard sleep that night, on Johnny's couch. At least the blankets kept me warm, but the sheep and goats made their bleats, broken with the calls of the llamas, and it kept me up. Bad dreams came with sleep. It was Thalia this time, riding on Butler—riding for the horizon. I followed her, but couldn't catch up. No matter how much I ran. Trying to outrun an elephant is a damn foolish thing to do—but in dreams, you commit all manner of foolish sins.

A bizarre face in the window greeted me as I woke up. A llama's round face, with delicate eyelashes and huge eyes, the wind playing about its fur. It looked so pleasant that I gave him a nod as I sat up. Then I grabbed my hat and vest and stumbled into my clothes.

"Johnny?" He wasn't about. The sun was high up, the clock in the corner saying that it was after ten. Maybe he was tending his flock? I went outside and pushed my way onto the porch.

There was Irish Johnny, standing before a line of horsemen. Making a sale. Morning mist clung to the hillside, making those horsemen look like ghosts who had ridden out of a scary story. They had a wagon with them, a buckboard pulled by a pair of camels, and two of their number hauled in crates of something or other and set them within.

I stepped off the porch and onto the grass, trying to get a better look at these buyers. One stared right back at me and I caught a glimpse of her face.

It was One-Eyed Ginny Wells.

She stared straight at me and I looked back. Then Johnny spun around and gave me a sharp look, a wave of his hand ordering me back into his house. He had a sale to make and I suppose I was wrecking it. Johnny had said that he sold armaments to outlaws. I didn't approve, but I couldn't stand in judgment on my host.

I went back into the house. Thalia was there, puttering around the kitchen. She'd already put some oats and milk in a bowl for Lady.

"Good morning, Corporal." She took a pot of coffee off the stove. "I trust you slept well? We should depart forthwith. Fort Fielding awaits."

"Yeah," I agreed. "That it does."

But I said it without eagerness.

CHAPTER SIX

WOLVES OF THE BORDERLANDS

We breakfasted with Irish Johnny before heading out for Fort Fielding. He wasn't much use in the kitchen, and I reckon he enjoyed Thalia's presence, and the ease with which she whipped up flapjacks and scrambled eggs. Afterwards, she went to the barn to prepare General Butler's breakfast—a mass of apples and vegetables mingled with hay and an entire water trough to wash it down—and Johnny and I walked onto the porch to say our farewells. The sun loomed above us, the sky pure blue and the prairie green tinged with frosty white. Winter had yet to truly start biting.

Johnny pointed to my waist. "You still carry the Cavalry Colt, boy-o? And the howdah gun? The buffalo rifle?"

"Yes, sir."

"Cavalry Colt's a gun of the past. You ought to get yourself a double-action. Carry a pair of them instead of the howdah—no, get yourself three. And a repeating rifle." He grimaced. "Matter of fact, you ought to take the damn Gatling gun I offered you."

"Why would I need that?"

"You're fighting an awful lot of people, ain't you?" He pointed to the barn as Thalia emerged, General Butler looming massive behind her. "She told me enough while you were paying a visit to the outhouse. My God—Orrin Prong. And all the martial might that commerce can supply. You need an army, Clarke."

"I'm dropping her off with Colonel MacDougal. It ain't my fight." I hesitated. "It ain't yours neither."

"Rufus Ridgeway was my friend!" He raised his voice. "And so are you." Hesitance in his voice—the sadness of a man who misses battle. Who misses a worthy cause. "You'll come to realize that. I know you will."

There's a special kind of hurt that comes from letting friends down. I felt it now.

I offered my hand. "Goodbye, Irish Johnny. I'll see you when I come round this way again."

"Aye." He clasped it as Thalia brought Butler about and tugged down the rope ladder. Ending his argument, now that she was close. "Farewell, colleen." He waved to her. "I'll be seeing you again. I know it."

"I look forward to it!" She waved to Irish Johnny as I headed over and clambered aboard. General Butler's trunk reached up and gave me a jab. He liked sleeping in a barn instead of the wilderness. Enjoyed fresh straw and nearly fresh fruit. The mammoth loved his comforts and was loathe to leave them.

We both had to do things that we didn't want to do.

Roundabout lunchtime, we arrived at Fort Fielding. This was the final outpost of America before the land of the Indian Nations—from the Black Hills and their mountains and the wide Dakota Plains and their surviving herds to the raging geysers around Yellowstone Lake. Everyone visiting the Nations, passing through, or leaving had to stop here, and it was as much town-sized trading post as military encampment. A wild conglomeration of ramshackle buildings, lean-tos, and tents surrounded the stout stockade, packed with Indians, hunters, soldiers, and tradesmen.

Thalia and I dismounted and led General Butler right down the middle. Just making sure he didn't step on anyone's toes wasn't easy, for folks in Fort Fielding didn't seem afraid of mammoths or anything else. In fact, the stalls and shouting merchants had numerous critters and pieces of critters for sale. One offered wolf pups and tiger cubs in cages, while another had a racing cheetah on offer, tongue lolling in his mouth as his long limbs stretched in the cold sun.

General Butler was far from the only mammoth. They trundled down the lanes and alleys. All sorts and sizes. Military mammoths of the Elephantry with blue and gold stitching on their howdahs and neatly combed fur. Mastodons brought in by the Natives, hauling pelts for sale. Canadians with their long, curl-tusked Woolies, come down to visit one of the United States' last outposts.

Plenty of mammoth ivory too.

Thalia was astounded, her eyes taking in all the roughness and beauty—the panoply of frontier chaos. I focused on getting to the big arched entrance of the fort, where Colonel MacDougal doubtlessly waited. Just putting one foot in front of the other.

Thalia nudged. "Corporal."

"Not now, goddamn it."

"Take a look over there. By the fellow selling corn." She whispered it. Like a professional.

I took a look. There was Marshal Bass Reeves, giving the cobs a sniff and chatting with the proprietor. Had he noticed us? Mammoths weren't exactly small, but there were plenty out here. And if he did see us, had he realized that I'd fed him a falsehood? I didn't fancy another meeting. Hopefully, he was so engrossed in conversation that he wouldn't notice one particular mammoth amongst the others trudging around the outskirts of the fort. I tapped Butler's foot and led him the other way, through an intersection. We'd skirt around Marshal Reeves and not disturb him.

So we did. Taking the longer way, and coming to another lane stocked with ramshackle businesses.

A caged bear roared. No ordinary beast—a Short-Faced Bear. Bears of all varieties, from the fearsome Grizzly to the mighty Polar of the north, were mere children compared to this ursine behemoth. Iron bars kept his long arms, snubbed muzzle bursting with teeth, and shaggy dark fur away from a growing audience. His eyes, each in a ring of lemon-colored fur, darted about, and a plaintive growl left his lips as his paws jabbed against the bars.

"By God, he is magnificent. I intend to make him mine." A familiar voice, oozing with arrogance. I tore my eyes away from the massive caged beast and there he was—A.B. Mulberry. It felt odd, seeing him there with the gold chain on his waistcoat and bowler hat, flanked by two Bracewell Detective guards. Like seeing the devil taking a stroll. He motioned to the bear's owner, a short Comanchero doing business far north. "Name your price, sir. I will not waste time in haggling."

My eyes went to Thalia. He hadn't spotted us and we could slip away without trouble. That would be the smart play. But the smart play was something Thalia rarely did. "Murderer!" She bellowed the word, stepping out of General Butler's shadow and advancing on Mulberry and the caged bear. I hurried after her, grabbing her arm. Lady capered about in circles, whickering madly. "You killed my father—you—you fiend!"

Mulberry's mouth quivered below his moustache. But that was the limit of his reaction. "Why, I did no such thing." Around him, the crowd shuffled and stared. Embarrassed and confused. In its cage, the Short-Faced Bear seemed to take in the growing outrage and pushed its mouth against the cage, tongue licking the bars. Butler snorted and stomped a foot. "The child has taken leave of her senses."

"That she has." I linked eyes with Mulberry. His two guards bristled. "I'll take her in hand and we'll be on our way. Apologies, sir." His gaze shot back—promising doom. Well, let him promise. But not with Thalia around.

"Corporal, this is our chance!" Thalia looked at me and then raised her voice, addressing the crowd. "He is a conspirator. He wishes to provoke war…"

I tightened my grip on her arm. "For God's sake, quit your yapping!"

One of the detectives strode closer, coat sliding back to reveal one of them fancy long-barreled Volcanic pistols at his hip. "She asking for trouble." He had a sallow, puff-lipped face that put me in mind of a catfish, with dewy glassy eyes and wisps of a moustache.

Just looking at him made me angry, and I forgot about the better part of valor. "Trouble's what you're gonna get, friend. Like your two buddies back in St. Louis." Even though it was Wild Bill who did for them—but the threat still had some iron in it.

"Bastard…" He snarled.

"Easy there, Mr. Brandt." Mulberry cut in. "The good corporal was just leaving."

But before we could make good our escape, a sort of ripple came through the crowd and they parted like the Red Sea before Moses. No prophet came to the fore to occupy the circle of dust before the bear cage. Instead, it was a soldier—a colonel, recognizable instantly by all concerned. That famous head of long blonde hair, now in thinner wafts and with stripes of gray in the matching moustache. A noticeable limp, his right foot at a miserable angle. A cane of mammoth ivory helped him walk, the head carved into the face of an eagle.

Colonel George Armstrong Custer.

"What's the meaning of this?" He stood tall, despite his limp. "This ruckus outside of my fort?"

Thalia spoke up first. "Colonel Custer. Thank heavens." She stepped closer to him. "That man, Mr. Mulberry, is a murderer and conspirator and…"

He brought up his cane and swung it down, sending a rain of gravel into the air. "You seem to be the one causing trouble. Accusing innocent folks." His gaze settled on me. "Threatening violence in the shadow of the Red, White, and Blue. Who are you, sir?"

While he spoke, I risked a glance at Mulberry. Total calm in the railroad man's half-closed eyes. Thalia's accusations might as well be a new rendition of 'Ol' Dan Tucker' for all the good they did. It meant one thing: he knew Custer would back him. Which meant Custer was in on it.

I answered, knowing there wasn't much I could do about it. "Corporal

Clement Clarke. Used to ride with the Elephantry."

"But you ride with those elephant ticks, no longer. So are you deserter or a coward?" He shook his head. "You certainly look like coward to me, who would flee when we have the greatest need of soldiers. And the girl." His eyes settled on Thalia. "No white blood in her. Chinese, I believe. A pair of troublemakers. Seems to me like a stay in the stockade is in order. Until we can figure out what's what."

His two cavalrymen stepped closer to enforce his will. They looked like no soldiers I had ever seen. Mangy and rumpled, with unshaven faces and their forage caps askew. One had a saber-tooth necklace dangling over his belly, the other had scalps on his belt. I could probably take them both—but not them and the two Bracewell boys. Not to mention the fact that gunning down cavalrymen outside a cavalry fort was probably a surefire way to get myself killed.

"Clarke! Clarke—there you are!" Another voice, back on the main road. The Short-Faced Bear roared in answer, and Butler started toward the new arrival, stretching out his trunk to greet an old friend. "And General Butler! Good to see you too, old man." My old friend, Colonel Mortimer MacDougal, almost lost in Butler's embrace.

Colonel Custer pushed up the brim of his hat to stare at MacDougal. "You know this deserter?" Not a trace of respect in his voice.

"That I do, Colonel. And he's no deserter." MacDougal filled his voice with bonhomie as he clasped my hand, but there was worry in it. "The girl too—Rufus Ridgeway's girl, I take it." Beneath his massive mutton chops, thick enough for a mammoth to hide in, his face was worried. "I'll take responsibility for them."

Thalia gave him a sunny smile. "Thank you, colonel."

"Think nothing of it." He pointed to the fort. "We'll go to my office. Give you a proper welcome."

"Hold on just a moment." Custer bristled. "They seem untrustworthy and yet you intend to take them—and their mammoth—into Fort Fielding to…"

"Former Corporal Clarke is many things, but he is trustworthy." MacDougal was already starting back toward the gates of the fort. "And you may be a cavalry colonel, but Fort Fielding is mine. You do not have the power to counter my order. Take it up with General Crook, if you disagree." He waved us to follow. General Butler already traipsed after him, trunk twisting happily. "Stand back, Colonel. You wouldn't want to get trampled."

Custer's face went red enough to match the glowering sun above. MacDougal knew to strike him where it hurt.

I doffed my hat to him and the same to Mulberry. They watched us all the way into the gates of Fort Fielding, their minds probably whirring along with plans of malice and skullduggery. It mattered little to me. My trail had reached its end.

Fort Fielding was the same as most military encampments that I'd had the misfortune to visit during my career. Armories, stables, and barracks neatly laid out behind the tall walls, with off-duty soldiers passing the time with cards or old letters while the officers drained whiskey in their club in the corner and their wives and children tried to put a little normalcy to all the death-dealing power arrayed and ready for use. The whole place stank of unwashed men and mammoth dung.

MacDougal motioned to a tall barn and corral on the other corner, where five mammoths munched on corn. "The General can join our shavetails. It would do them good to be in the company of a veteran." He grinned as we walked to an adobe structure, unfortunately downwind from the mammoths. "We have access to some truly fine animals. You should give them a look, Clarke. I've got a Woolly of Canadian stock that belongs on the stage in a County Fair."

"And I bet you never have to struggle to find grub for them." I motioned Butler over to the corral, where a quartet of stable-hands waited to pamper him. He trumpeted in happiness and I waved back. "Fine times in the Elephantry, eh?"

His face darkened. "Let's talk in my office. Come along, Thalia."

He closed the door behind us and had us sit before a crooked desk covered in untidy papers. Framed photographs of the old days covered the walls, along with his mounted saber. I looked at one. Me, Irish Johnny, Rufus Ridgeway, and MacDougal.

God, how had we been so young?

Thalia sat on the chair and he poured her water from a jug. "You're all right, Miss Ridgeway? You're not tired or hungry? I can grant you a fine bed in the guest quarters and a good meal from the mess." He smiled at her nervously.

"Thank you, but I'm quite well." She was on pins and needles as well. "Colonel, I must warn you—there is a terrible conspiracy afoot. My father..."

"I know," MacDougal said.

"My father died to..." She stopped. "What?"

"Mulberry's scheme. I know." He weaved his hands through his fading dark curls and smoothed down his massive sideburns. "Your father, Miss Ridgeway, wrote to me soon after Mulberry visited him. I was worried, to say the least. And so, I did some digging." He drummed his fingers on the table. "Mulberry's concern, fueled by the money of railroads and industrialists, has purchased friends of numerous local politicians, all of whom began urging war with the Nations. And then there's our friend outside. The good Colonel Custer."

"He's with Mulberry," I said. "I'd bet Butler on it."

"He's an American soldier!" Thalia picked up Lady and smoothed down her mane. "How could he dishonor the flag by—by plotting such an unjust war?"

MacDougal sighed. "He wants another engagement—wants revenge for the defeat Crazy Horse gave him at the Little Bigtusk. He wants revenge for his leg. I doubt Mulberry paid him at all. He simply proposed and Custer listened. But Mulberry certainly paid for the special weaponry for Custer's private band of soldiers—he calls them his Immortals. A collection of scalp-hunters and mammoth poachers who got their start butchering Cheyenne women and children at the Washita."

"And these Immortals—they'll be the ones to start the war?"

"It's quite likely." He leaned back in his seat. "I've brought up the issue. Wrote to congressmen and generals. They've expressed interest, but its gone no further than that. Either Mulberry's bought them off or they agree with him and want the Indian Nations destroyed. And why wouldn't they? Manifest Destiny has brought our nation from the plains of Texas to the shore of California. Why should a grand chunk in the center remain untouched?"

"But you don't agree?" I asked.

"No. I've seen war, Clement. Just like you. I do not hunger for it." He lowered his head.

"How will they do it? How will they make the trumpets sound?"

MacDougal leaned back in his chair. "I need to know—and I don't. Right now, we have a sort of unofficial truce. No full call to the battle, but not a true peace either. So they'll need to create some sort of incident. Perhaps if some peace envoys are attacked, forcing the hands of the Nations. Or if they can prove that the Indian Nations launched an attack on American soldiers—even if it was in self-defense, in their territory—that could justify launching a grand conflict." He smirked. "Worked with Mexico, I suppose."

"Well, you're ready for it, ain't you?" I wondered. "So you can stop it? When it happens."

His eyes went sad. "I simply don't know."

Thalia let out a little sob, though no tears marked her face. This was it. We'd traveled all the way across the country, braving countless dangers to reach Colonel MacDougal, and he could do nothing to help us. Mulberry's money had bought him victory.

I felt pretty low. And lower still as I took a step toward the door.

"Corporal?" Thalia asked. "You're leaving?"

I held my Stetson in my hands. "I did what I told you I was gonna do. I brought you to Colonel MacDougal. He'll keep you safe from Mulberry and Prong." I gave the door a nudge with my boot. "Better than I can."

MacDougal glared up at me from the desk, eyes like the last hot coals in the fire. "You intend to flee?" A quiver ran through his cheeks, making his sideburns shake. "It's a dangerous situation, to say the least. But I can use you."

"You could?" I demanded. "A rundown mammoth rider?"

"Goddamn it, man!" He sputtered. "This is Ridgeway's daughter. Private Ridgeway, corporal, who…"

"I'm a drunk!" I nearly shouted the words. "And a scoundrel. A no-account bounty hunter. A dissolute rambler. A sinner." The vehemence faded. "I can't look after Thalia. Can't hardly look after myself. Whatever plan you compose will be better for my absence." I turned. Facing that office was too much. "Farewell, Colonel. Farewell, Thalia."

She left the chair. Ran to me and put her arms around mine. Tears shone on her cheeks. "Reconsider. Please."

I pulled away and stumbled outside. I had abandoned her, as promised. Now, I wanted to get drunk.

General Butler could stay in the stables in the fort, until I decided to leave. They'd look after him, let him dine on the finest hay that American tax dollars could purchase, and I'd pick him up and ride him out when I was ready to leave. And go where? Damned if I knew. Maybe ride down south, give Texas a try. Make my way into Mexico, lay out in the sun and drink tequila while betting on the Terror Bird fights. Or maybe I'd go to California. Or the North Pole.

For the moment, I needed to be away from Fort Fielding. Some prospector's wagon rolled eastwards and I hopped aboard—I'd find a similar way back in the dark, or just sleep where I drank—and let it carry me away from the great stockade and the cluster of settlement. Further on, we came to a lean-to saloon and trading post built into the side of a hill. It was the place where a sodbuster could drown his sorrows after the farm failed. Perfect for me.

I pushed through the flap of tanned sloth hide that served as the door and headed to the counter. Only a little light from a dangling lantern, casting shadows on the dirt floor and planks of rough-hewn wood that served as counter and furniture. The bartender had a massive beard that appeared to encompass his entire body, and a pet capybara jabbing his muzzle in a bowl of milk. It was a contest as to who stank the worst. Besides me and the capybara, there was no one else inside.

"What'll it be?" the barkeep asked.

"Rotgut, friend." I settled down, paying with the remainder of the cash I'd gotten from Thalia's terrible grandparents. "And keep it coming."

He filled a dirty glass and I drank it. The booze settled hot and painful in the bottom of my stomach. I had another. A third and I'd be over the edge and plummeting into the abyss, which suited me fine. There was a kind of happiness in the lack of responsibility, a joy in the ability to do what you wanted, when you wanted, and not have some nagging voice in the back of your mind telling you to do otherwise. Had not that impulse filled the barrooms and gambling halls of America? I'd been happy before Thalia arrived. Why couldn't I conjure that joy again?

The flap rustled. "Howdy." It was Wild Bill Hickok—my old friend. A fine surprise. He crossed the dirt floor and joined me. "May I join you?"

"Drinking with a friend is always preferable to drinking alone. By all means." I pointed to the crate next to me and he sat down. He ordered a drink and we sat together in the darkness. "What brings you north?"

"I don't know. Seems as good as any place. You take care of that girl?"

"Dropped her at the fort with an old comrade. She'll be okay." Or I hoped she would. "Oh—I ran into Cody a little bit south." Cody and Hickok were friends and he might be keen to hear the news. "Seems Buffalo Bill's taking a respite from the theatre and is now working as a hunting guide. He was showing a fancy-pants aristocrat around. Letting him play mammoth hunter."

"Sheeeit." Hickok whistled. "He mentioned that, when we was touring the stage in New York. Said that it was damn good publicity for his shows and the dime novels they was writing about him. That fool Buntline, with his scribbling." He brushed his long, perfumed hair back from his narrow face. "What is becoming of us, Clarke? We are like your mammoths. Either we learn to perform in circuses or we—we…" He stopped and ended his words with a slug of whiskey.

"We what?"

He fixed me with his cold glare once more. "We go extinct."

The door rustled. Hickok froze, the whiskey still in one hand, the other at his belt. It was gunfighter instinct. I went still as well, and the bartender ducked down as a line of fading sunlight crept into the saloon.

Then Mulberry's voice filled the gloom. "That's him. At the bar—and his associate." He'd tracked me here—though he didn't risk going inside. And he wasn't alone.

Goddamn it, I was done with this. I spun around. "Mulberry, I'm through with it. I'm done. Will you not simply let a man get drunk in peace?"

He ignored me. "Get him out of there. Post-haste."

"We sat together in the darkness."

Hickok stared into his drink. "You do know who I am, do you not?"

Brandt, the Bracewell Detective from earlier. "Mr. Mulberry—that's—that's Wild Bill Hickok..." All the bravado he'd shown before had vanished. Wild Bill had that effect on people.

"I don't give a damn if it's the Angel Gabriel. Kill them both. You have the mastodon. Now, I'm needed elsewhere." He raised his voice. "Goodbye, Corporal Clarke." A mastodon? Oh Lord, what did that mean? They'd brought a war elephant?

Mulberry didn't care that I'd given up the fight. He still wanted me dead. And my friend too "Wild Bill..."

"You go over the bar." He finished his whiskey. "Shelter there. Back me up a bit, if you can and then slip on out the back."

"Bill..."

He set the glass down as nervous feet stepped toward the flap and stood, gripping both the revolvers in his sash. He raised his voice, shouting to the Bracewell boys as they hastened in to put an end to us both. "Good evening, gentlemen. Glad to have you here. We're going to the devil together." Then he spun and drew, faster than they could fire.

Both his revolvers roared together. The Bracewell man in the doorway toppled back, shot twice. Blood settled on the dirt. The capybara squealed madly and went scrambling to the corner. I wished to hell I could join him. A rifle jabbed through the little window and Hickok shot the man behind it, hitting his target perfectly.

I pulled my way over the bar and dropped down, taking cover. Doing as I was told. Hickok looked back at me. "It's all right, Clarke. You've been a good friend to me. This is all I could ask for—and far better than I might have gotten." He was smiling.

Then another shot punched through the flap and caught Wild Bill low in the gut. It ripped the flap away, giving us all a look at what waited outside. A firing line of Bracewell gunmen—at least a dozen of them. Behind them, outlined in the setting sun, a mastodon—equipped for war. It wore a suit of armor, the sort that would bedeck a knight's warhorse in an old storybook, with gaps for its trunk and tusks. On the back, a miniature cannon waited, with a blue-coated crew to man it. Custer's Immortals, no doubt.

Wild Bill looked back at me. He smiled. "Adios."

Then he stepped outside and kept shooting.

"No!" I cried after him as his pistols flashed and the Bracewell guns answered him. Two of them dropped in the first second, and a third fell, and Hickok was shaking all the while, the bullets ripping through his fancy buckskin duds and boots and spattering his blood every which way. The cannon on the mastodon fired and the whole front of the saloon vanished in a cloud of fire, splinters, and dust.

The bartender scrambled out of his hiding place and ran toward the back of the dugout, grabbed my arm, and hauled me along. “Come on, partner.” He had his capybara tucked under one arm. “Got me a tunnel leads out the back.”

“Bill!” I tried to pull free.

“He’s gone, friend.” The barman’s eyes were sad. “You gotta let him go.”

This time, I went.

We slipped down a little door worked in the dirt and then through a dingy tunnel. Maybe they’d built it as a place to hide and escape from Indians. Now, it saved us. We made our way through the tunnel until its ending, in a little grassy hillside a way’s from the bar. The hairy barkeep and I emerged like prairie dogs into the cool night air.

I gazed back at the saloon.

The front was all wreckage. The armored mastodon loomed over it, one of its crew lying dead at its feet. A few more corpses around it—the last men killed by Wild Bill. And there he was—knocked on his side, blasted apart, and somehow still trying to stand, pick up his pistols, and fire again. A barrage came from the surrounding Bracewell boys. Clouds of gunpowder drifted up.

Wild Bill was dead.

Next to me, the bartender set down the capybara. He knelt down and petted the creature, soothing it with gentle words and the click of his tongue. “You all right there?” Was he talking to me or the capybara? “There’s a trail, past that patch of sage. It’ll join the main road and lead you to Fort Fielding. Though it’s a bit of a walk. You start now, you can reach the safety of the fort.”

“And you? You’ll be all right?”

“I got kin nearby. I’ll stay with them. Reckon it’ll be safer than staying in town.”

“You’re like my guardian angel.” I checked my pockets. Not much left. I gave him some folding money—it hardly seemed enough. “Sorry about your place.”

“That was just soil and booze. Not so hard to rebuild. Besides, you’re a customer. Them bastards blew up my saloon didn’t even knock. But I’m not your guardian angel.” Sadness in his voice. “That honor belongs to the man who saved both of us.” He spoke-sung a few sad words—a cowboy ballad. “Beat the drum slowly and play the fife lowly.”

“Yeah.”

I lowered my head. I mourned a legend. I mourned a friend.

Just like that old barkeep said, the trail doubled around and led back to Fort Fielding. I could make out the outline of the place, a black rectangle over the gentle rise. The silhouette faded as darkness deepened. Up above, a few chunks of frost danced their way down and I shivered in my vest. No sign of the Bracewell killers. No sign of anyone on that lonely trail. I had time to think.

Revenge. That need was gnawing at me, but something else was too—I'd felt that way before. After those border ruffians killed my pa, vengeance had filled me up. It had kept me going throughout that horrible war, past God only knew how many travails and dangers, and when the last battle ended, the revenge just dried up. Left me bereft and weak. Dry and brittle as a tumbleweed, blown about by the prairie winds.

But fate had offered me something else. It had put a child into my path, and though I spurned her, Thalia Ridgeway cared for me still. A child, and a fine cause.

Wild Bill had given his life to keep me alive. His death had struck like a passing roll of thunder. It seemed absurd. How could a man like that die? You might as well imagine the mountains dead, or the streams or the sky. And yet, he was gone, and all for my sake. What could I do to honor him?

The answer came to me.

Something cold trickled down the back of my neck. I turned around. A dire wolf, black of fur and silver of eye, loomed at the edge of the grass. He was an ancient beast, one eye turned milky, an ear half gnawed away, and scars crossing his fur. His tail went up as he matched my pace, walking along the road. I stared past him, watching for the rest of the pack—but they were nowhere to be found.

He was a lone wolf. No wonder there was a limp to his lope and he bore so many scars. In this world, lone wolves don't last long.

I had a means to avoid that fate. Someone to help, and a cause: stop Mulberry. Put an end to him and his scheme. Protect Thalia.

I put my finger to the brim of my hat. "Obliged to you."

He turned around and vanished, bushy tail wagging as he hid himself in the grass.

It was the rattle of a wagon that had scared him. I spun around. More enemies? No—a familiar sight. The Ambulatory Arcanum, with a pair of green-tinted lanterns attached to its front and the pygmy mammoth tugging the odd conveyance along. Professor Ashe gripped the reins, young Maximilian next to him—sleeping the untroubled sleep of a tired child. He slowed the wagon and it came to a creaking halt before me.

I removed my hat. "Professor Ashe. Can I trouble you for a ride?"

"That depends. What is your destination?"

"Fort Fielding." I hesitated. Sending him into danger wasn't right. "Actually, maybe I better walk and you better roll somewhere else. Marshal Reeves is there, looking for you."

"Oh, fear not—I have it on good authority that he's already ridden to the west, into the Indian Nations." He tapped his fez as if it was an outgrowth of an oversized brain. "Rumors, carefully spread, told him that we had ridden that way. He's doubtlessly riding west as we speak. Once again, my cunning has prevailed." He patted the seat next to him, stirring young Maximilian into wakefulness. "I'd be honored to give you a ride."

Well, if he said so. I scrambled up and plopped down. Dust still covered my vest and cap and I was shaking a bit from the exchange of lead. Professor Ashe gave the reins a crack and little Goliath started his progress down the road. Dust came in torrents as we went up a gentle rise, giving us a better look at Fort Fielding. Up above, a fading moon winked down—a callous eye, lost in the frost.

Ashe seemed right pleased with himself for his deception. "Yes, sir—that schnorrer Reeves made a mistake when he set his sights on Professor Ashe. Max!" He flicked the tired, yawning boy into weak wakefulness. "Take heed, *boychick*. Brain will always beat brawn. That's why our species has triumphed over the mammoth and the ground sloth. The cunning ploy will always..."

Marshal Bass Reeves rode his charger out of the chaparral, right into our path. He hoisted up a lantern with one hand, and drew out his shotgun with the other.

Ashe stilled the reins. Goliath gave a weary trumpet and squeaked to a halt. We froze before the burning eyes of the Marshal.

"First you lied to me down in Kansas, Corporal Clarke." Reeves hoisted the lantern, adding a gleam to his keen eyes. "Then I catch wind of more lies over here—rumors that the great Professor Ashe and his snake oil has lit out for the Indian Nations. Hoping to peddle his codswallop to the tribes, maybe." He spat on the ground. "You two must take me for a fool."

Things were getting bad, and I needed to get to the fort. "Reeves—leave him be. I beg of you."

"A bounty hunter ought not to dictate the law."

"There's more outlaws. Plenty more. Some wearing union blue and trying to start a war." I swallowed and started laying out the details of the conspiracy. "Colonel Custer himself is a part of it. He's going to launch some attack, blame it on the Lakota. Brew up battle that will fill cemeteries to the bursting." Clutching at straws—that summed up my desperate effort. "I know you got no reason to believe me, after I lied to you before..."

"There's some truth."

"But you got to, sir. For Thalia's sake. That's the girl I was with. The little one I was looking after. She's there in the fort and I have to help her."

"Thalia?" Young Max had been looking from his uncle to the marshal with a mix of fear and wonder—but now fear and concern took over. "Thalia's in danger?"

"I'm afraid so."

He tugged at his uncle's sleeve. "We have to help her, Uncle—we must!"

Reeves watched, impassive. "Maybe you got these two playing along. Maybe you're telling the truth." He kept his eyes trained on the professor. "Don't change the fact that Professor Ashe is a swindler and needs to face Judge Parker."

"He will." It was Maximilian who spoke up. The boy's voice shook. "He'll face justice. He'll do the right thing, I promise. But first, we need to help Thalia." He was scared, but speaking anyway. "Please, Mr. Reeves. Can we help her?"

If a mouse of a boy could risk everything, then why couldn't I? It was nice to hear Max speak up. Told me I was on the right course.

Reeves thought it over for a few long seconds. Snow danced overhead. Then he pointed to the professor. "We'll go to Fort Fielding. Check on the girl. Then, he'll come with me to the see the Judge."

"He will…" Maximilian started.

"I need to hear him say it."

Professor Ashe sighed. "Your parents taught you well." He removed his fez, revealing his little Hebrew cap. "Yes. I'll face my justice. After this."

"You sure will. I ain't leaving your side." Reeves turned his horse around. "Come on back to the fort. Don't even think of running."

We didn't.

It was well-past midnight when we returned to Fort Fielding. The place ought to be settling down to sleep, with only unlucky sentries up and watching the prairie. Instead, it was in an uproar. Torches and lanterns blazing, men getting horses and camels ready and lowering down the loading platform for the Elephantry. Soldiers stood in shuffling clusters, readying their rifles and warming their hands over campfires. A flash of Reeves' badge got us through the gate.

We rode in, and there was Thalia, standing near the mammoth corral. She was bundled up, only a smidge of her face showing amongst her big coat, hat, and scarf, and she waved to us with a mitten. Ashe drove the wagon right over. She pulled down her scarf and her smile lit up the world.

Thank God—Mulberry hadn't risked attacking her in the midst of so many soldiers.

"Corporal Clarke!" She clasped my hand. "You came back!"

"I did. Now what's going on?"

"A messenger came in. Lakota messenger." She pointed to the longhouse in the center of the fort. "The officers—they're talking about what to do. Colonel MacDougal's there. And so is Custer."

I had to hear it. "Thalia, you see if you can get these others settled." I swung down from the coachman's seat. "I'll go and have a listen."

"I'm coming with you," Reeves added. "Gotta see this business for myself."

No time for arguments from anyone. We crossed the scrum of solders, cavalrymen, and dismounted elephantry, and went straight to the longhouse.

A soldier stood guard and I went tall and fixed him with a glare that belonged to the meanest sergeant I could remember. A little gasp appeared on his pimply face and he snapped off a salute, which I returned. "They need you on the battlements—get moving!"

"Sir..." he started.

"I don't remember saying you could ask questions, boy—get moving!" I bellowed it loud enough that my lack of uniform didn't matter. He vamoosed.

The door opened quietly and Reeves and I slid inside. Inside, the officers of Fort Fielding sat at a long table, cups of coffee steaming in front of them. Custer was there, his ruined leg jutting out. So was MacDougal—and even Reverend Allen Allensworth, who had saved our bacon back down south.

MacDougal spotted me and motioned me over. Reeves went too. Amongst all the soldiers, a few still in their civilian garb since they'd been hauled in from the outskirts, we didn't stand out so badly.

Reeves flashed his badge. "Marshal." A courtly nod from MacDougal.

"Colonel," Reeves replied—recognizing the rank.

At the head of the table sat General George Crook, with his two great wiry triangles of beard. He'd commanded me when I was with the Elephantry after the war, during my time as an Indian Fighter. A good man, as I remembered him, and if he wasn't equal to the task that history so often gave him, well—who was? Now, he examined a piece of neatly-written paper through a pair of tiny spectacles.

He removed them and let the paper fall. "They mean to treat with us."

"Who?" Custer demanded.

"The Indians—what's who." He tapped the paper. "This was written by a fellow calling himself Carlos Montezuma. That's no war chief I've ever heard of, but he writes like a scholar and says he speaks for Crazy Horse and Sitting Bull and the rest. And they wish to meet and present their demands."

MacDougal listened carefully. "And what is the nature of these demands?"

"In short, that we respect their borders, and keep out poachers and prospectors. In return, they'll offer trade, allow some to enter, and promise peace." He removed the spectacles. "They're sending out a delegation to meet in Elephant Head, the old Ghost Town. We are to send our own, to meet them."

"Delegation." Custer spat. "It's a Redskin ruse, to make us send our manpower to one place while they attack another. They can no more make peace than they can properly make war—those are attributes of civilized nations." He tapped his cane against the floorboards. "Let my soldiers—my Immortals—go out and meet them. We'll cut down all their assorted war parties."

"You're so eager for another Little Bigtusk, Custer?" MacDougal asked.

"Side-burned snake! I'll thrash you right now!"

Gruff arguments followed, and Custer had to be held back. Crook sighed and rested his head in his hands. "Reverend." He looked to Allensworth. "You've been here long enough. What do you think?"

Allensworth had lit his pipe. "The Indians aren't the sort to play tricks. If they say they want peace, then that's what they want. And you have to consider what a war will be like—they're the finest mammoth riders on God's earth. They've been arming themselves too. Weaponry purchased from the *Syndicat Metis* up north and smuggled across the border. And it would take a great deal of time for reinforcements to join us from back east. We would win, in the end—but it would be a hard-fought war indeed. If this delegation is not received, that is. And all under your watch, sir."

Crook nodded. "Fair enough." He stood. "All right. Here's what we'll do. I'll send word to Bismarck. The senator's in town. He can hear their demands and carry them to Washington." Custer started to complain and Crook waved him silent. "Your 'Immortals,' can ride out as pickets. Don't get near Elephant Head—just establish a perimeter. You hear me, Custer? Don't start a fight you can't win."

Custer saluted. "Yes, sir."

It was all the chance he needed. Either he'd attack those chiefs or he'd let Mulberry's mercenaries slip in and do it for him. The results would be the same—the Indians had sought peace and been attacked. They'd go to war against every target they could find, perhaps even wipe out Fort Fielding, the United States would answer, and the Nations would be wiped away. A tide of blood would cover the prairies. Mulberry would get his plains cleared for the railroad. He'd win.

Colonel MacDougal sighed. "Well, there you have it." We joined the crowd of officers, filing out of the hall and back into the snowy darkness. MacDougal trailed after Clarke and myself.

We crossed the courtyard to the stockade, to where Thalia and the others waited. She had Lady tucked in her arms and General Butler above her, his trunk reaching down and playing about her shoulder—he was glad to have her along. But the look on my face told Thalia, Ashe, and little Maximilian that trouble was coming.

"Young Monty sent notice of a peace delegation. They're coming up, want to meet in Elephant Head—the old Ghost Town." I told them the rest. Custer's determination for war, and Crook letting him ride out with pickets. "That means he's gonna attack them at Elephant Head while they wait. Or Mulberry will—antagonizing them with his mercenaries, and then Custer will be riding to the defense of a respectable private citizen. Saving the day and getting his glory and war in one fell swoop."

Reeves pointed to MacDougal. "You're wearing blue. Could you help?"

MacDougal looked miserable. "If I brought my mammoths out, I'd be disobeying a direct order. Playing right into Custer's hands."

Thalia listened carefully. "But we are not soldiers. So, we can get there first. And defend the Indian envoys."

She said it so simply. Get there first and defend them. Easy as picking up some flour from the general store.

I couldn't help grinning. "Darling—they'll have a whole company..."

"We have General Butler." She looked fondly at the mammoth. "And Professor Ashe—could we make use of your services? I promise that Max will be safe. Marshal Reeves, we could certainly use your help. Provoking war with a neighboring nation during a ceasefire—does that not break the law? If you would assist us, I would be forever in your debt."

"Forever in my debt, huh?" he asked.

Ashe, for once, was speechless.

"Thalia." I started. "I came back to help you. But going up against that many guns..."

"You came back," she said. "I knew you would. And you'll save this land from tyranny. That's the kind of man you are."

I looked at Butler. Those dark eyes, bursting with wisdom, stared right back. He was braver than I could ever hope to be. He'd stand with Thalia, because he cared for her. It wasn't the care of a dog for their owner or a horse for their rider. A deeper intelligence filled the minds of mammoths. But they loved just as deep and they cared just as much. The General wanted to protect her, and I knew that I did too.

"I'll ride with you," I said.

Reeves laughed. "Reckon I will too. After what I've heard, I've got to." He swung back onto his horse. "Come on. I know the road to Elephant Head.

We've got to get there before this Mulberry fellow does."

MacDougal watched us, hardly noticing the frost clinging to his mutton chops. "This is—this is utter insanity. I suppose I'll talk to Allensworth, see if I can get you some help."

Utter insanity. That was so. But there was no time for cowardice or worry or even many preparations. I helped Thalia open the corral and hopped inside. The smaller pachyderms shuffled back, giving warning grunts and trumpets. Butler came out and bowed and I made it up onto his back. Professor Ashe had taken Maximilian out to get his wagon. Thalia went up the rope ladder, and then we were ready to ride.

To ride to battle.

CHAPTER SEVEN

A GOOD DAY TO DIE

Somewhere along the road, all dark and cold and bathed in shadow, we came across a buckboard wagon rolling our way. General Butler noted it first, his trunk arching, and I reached back for my buffalo rifle. The buckboard sat on the side of the road, pulled by a pair of mules, with a lantern on a stick near the front. A hand waved to us. I had Butler take a few cautious steps closer.

Marshal Reeves was less patient. "Who's there?" He reached for his shotgun. "Show yourself or face the consequences!"

"You're riding with a marshal now?" Irish Johnny. His brogue cut through the darkness as he stood up in the seat. Someone was with him, a figure in a hat trimmed with feathers and a faded Union greatcoat. I recognized her—and the saber-toothed tiger that stalked his way from the side of the wagon and sat on his haunches near the terrified mules. "It's only me. And you know Miss Hewitt, I'm sure."

Lenora Hewitt sat there, her rifle with the spyglass on her shoulder. She reached down and Butterscotch pressed his head and back against her palm—a giant housecat using a human hand to pet himself. "Looks like you've got some friends, corporal. Is that Marshal Reeves, I see?"

"Still waiting for the day I'm sent after you, Hewitt." He made his reply with a smile.

"And I am Professor Alexander Ashe, at your service." Ashe made a show of doffing his fez. "Mendicant mystic, wandering wonder-worker, peregrine purveyor of…" No one paid him much heed.

I couldn't believe it. "What are y'all doing here?"

"We came to help you, you big idiot." Johnny gave one of his famous grins. "Miss Ridgeway told me about how you helped Hewitt down south in Jubilee. She and I met during the war—helped with some scouting. I sent her a telegram, and when she arrived, we started for the Indian Nations. Figured we'd cross paths."

"Doesn't really answer my question."

"Because you helped defend Jubilee," Hewitt said. "And I don't want to be in your debt."

"And I'm your friend, you addle-brained dullard." Johnny patted the buckboard. "And you've got to see what I brought along."

I considered arguing, until a phrase came to mind: the more, the merrier. Well, it wouldn't be merry where we were going. But we could use the firepower—and arguing with Irish Johnny and Lenora Hewitt seemed a foolish notion. I sighed. "All right. Join our procession. It's been a while since we were up here, but I don't think it's much longer until we reach Elephant Head."

"I ought to warn you about that." Johnny cracked the reins as Butterscotch rose to his feet. He was eyeing Goliath, the Ashe's pygmy mammoth—that beast would be a fine meal for him. "Took a look over there earlier. Some smoke was coming up. The ghost town's inhabited."

"Swell." I tightened my knees, making Butler resume his trot. "Let's go and find out who."

It could be any number of folks. Maybe the Indians, Sitting Bull, Crazy Horse, and young Carlos Montezuma, had arrived. Or maybe Mulberry's men had slipped in and were waiting in ambush. Only we'd fall victim instead of those Lakota Braves.

Well, I guess we'd find out soon enough. And it felt good to have some friends along for the ride.

The trail ended a little before dawn. Elephant Head. Before the wars of '76 and '77 had decided the matter, miners had poured in and built a settlement here, expecting to strike it rich from the gold of the Black Hills. Now, it was a ghost town—an empty set of ramshackle buildings, cabins, shacks, a single great hotel, and numerous saloons—all left to rot and ruin in the elements. Toys set down by a child and forgotten. Now, as the sun came blood red in the cold sky, we rode down the main street.

And there, in the middle, we came across one of the strangest sights I've ever witnessed in the West. There was a campfire, and the outlaws of the Ginny Wells Gang sat and prepared breakfast. Dirty Dave, the fellow with the lack of cleanliness, was playing a fiddle. The gentle, lilting tune of the Red

River Valley.

In front of him, a giant ground sloth stood. Those massive, long arms ending in huge claws. Sad, placid eyes surrounded by circles of white. Someone had given him an oversized coat made of a patchwork quilt, all different colors, and a big conical dunce cap sat on his head. The sloth was waving his arms back and forth, stomping his feet, and singing along with low, warbling squeaks and squeals.

Wells noticed us first.

She sprang up, going for the sawed-off on her hips—and then stopped. Her eyes went to Irish Johnny. Maybe I was a threat, but Johnny was a friend. Dirty Dave noticed our arrival next and the bow left his fiddle. That sloth in the costume did another swaying dance step and then he froze up too.

I leaned down from Butler. "Howdy."

"What the hell are you doing here?" Wells demanded.

"Could ask the same of you. Watching a waltzing sloth—what's that about?"

"I can tell you that. His name's Pierrot. We stole him from a traveling medicine show we robbed a day ago." Wells looked back at him. "Was thinking of turning him free, but all he knows to do is dance and wave his arms about for treats." Her hands went to her hip. "This town seemed a likely hideout. That's my explanation. What's yours?"

Irish Johnny spoke up before I could. "Tell me, Miss Wells, how'd you like to make a fortune in pilfered armaments? Maybe steal yourself a railroad man for a king's ransom? And all you have to do is give the guns of you and your gang a little play?"

Dirty Dave had tucked his fiddle under his arm. "What are you jawing about?"

Thalia cleared her throat. "A conspiracy. A grand conspiracy to drag our country into war. We can stop it—by stopping them." She gave an explanation. A quick one. I looked at the faces of the outlaws, seeking an answer as to what they'd do. Contrary to popular opinion, the average outlaw ain't in love with gun smoke. They like easy money—and this battle didn't strike me as easy.

Wells listened. "You'll be fighting alongside me, Corporal Clarke?"

"Afraid so."

"Huh." She looked back at her gang. "Anyone ain't interested can ride out. I'll think no less of you." Dirty Dave had already started to his horse, which waited at a hitching post there on the street. "Dave—you leave the fiddle. That's mine." Then she turned back. "You pay us in bullets and gunpowder and dynamite, Johnny. In advance. Just in case things don't work out."

He shrugged. "Fine with me."

"All right." Wells smoothed her hair back and walked closer, looking us over.

Her eye went to Professor Ashe, who waved weakly, then to Marshal Reeves, who was staring daggers, then to Lenora Hewitt, who gave her a quiet nod, and finally at me. "I suppose I owe you, Clarke. Strange as it sounds, you treated me right. Or at least, after this, you'll owe me. Now, you're the soldier. What ought we to do?"

I stood tall in General Butler's saddle and looked over our pathetic army. Half of Wells' gang was already riding away, dust rising from their hooves. That left six gunslingers, Lenora Hewitt and her fancy rifle and big kitty-cat, Marshal Reeves—who could take on an army, but not two of them—and Irish Johnny, who was no slouch either. Add Professor Ashe and his boy to that—who would be next to useless—and the volatile cargo they carried in their wagon. And Thalia.

And Butler and me.

That was all. Against Custer's Immortals and God only knew how many Bracewell killers, who had brought a mastodon in armor to the table. It just wasn't fair.

"Johnny, tell me you brought some nice toys in the wagon?"

"I got just the ticket," he agreed.

"Okay." I motioned to him and Lenora Hewitt. "You two are soldiers. Probably better heads at tactics than me. I tend to let General Butler plan all my military engagements. So let's hear your expertise. Mulberry and his men will be coming in soon. How we gonna beat them?"

Hewitt and Irish Johnny exchanged a glance. A few moments later, they started to plan.

Dawn came slowly this time of year. It crept out slow in the cold light and put down shafts of light the color of blood. They shone over the main street, where I stood—alone. Playing the role of bait. Ahead of me, a party of horsemen arrived, surrounding a great shiny lump. That was the armored mastodon. My spyglass let me have a look around. Further back, a few coaches lay in a circle. The caged short-faced bear sat in the center. I guess Mulberry had brought his souvenir along.

The Bracewell boys drew closer. They were mounted—probably a score of black-clad hardcases looking for a fight. Dust rose up from their hooves, creeping up in twisting clouds to match the fire in the sky. I stood alone, facing off with them, one hand on the iron at my hip and the other resting on the strap of my rifle. No one else was visible. Just me, staring down a pack of gunmen.

A smarter man wouldn't be there—and if he was, he'd piss himself. But I stood firm.

Orrin Prong rode at the head of the pack on a piebald mare, Mulberry next to him on a stately bay. Prong tugged at the reins, slowing, and drew his revolver. He aimed it right at me—giving me many seconds to look down that barrel as he rode up.

"Shoot him!" Mulberry nearly bellowed the words. "By God, what are you waiting for, man? Shoot that miscreant down."

Prong didn't even look at him. "There's some trickery here. Something's afoot. Like to know what it is." He raised his voice, calling to me. "You got something planned, Clarke? You and that half-pint accompanying you. Where is she?" He extended his pistol. "Tell me or the first one's going in your gut."

But as he did so, he rode closer. They all did—slowing to a walk. Their long guns swiveled about, aiming at those empty ghost town buildings. Everything in Elephant Head was a potential threat. Perfect place for an ambush, which they had doubtlessly been planning on. Still, no gunshot greeted them. No gunpowder howdy-do. And so, heedlessly, assured that their wariness would defend them, they rode in closer.

"Best start talking, Clarke," Prong commanded. "I am not a patient man."

"Cut him down!" Mulberry cried. "Cut him down and let's have an end to this!"

Still, I said nothing.

"Maybe you're right." Prong took aim. Impatient indeed. "Adios, Clement Clarke. Looks like you're dying alone."

They weren't close enough. Not all of them. But this was the best we were gonna get. I raised my voice. "Who said anything about alone?"

That was our edge. Mulberry knew about me and Thalia, but that was the limit of it. He didn't know about my friends and he didn't expect what was coming next.

Lenora Hewitt, One-Eyed Ginny, and Marshal Reeves, all on separate rooftops, hurled down bottles of Elohim Elixir. Each bottle had a rag in the stem, set afire. They crashed into the ranks of the Bracewell horsemen and shattered, glass and blazing liquid settling on everything. Men and horses rode every which way, screaming and firing their guns as roiling smoke and dust welled up like the earth itself was turning against them.

Prong fired and missed. Trying to steady your aim when there's a green fire bedlam ripping to life behind you is nearly impossible. I was already running, heading for the side street. There, beside the two-story Elephant Hotel, General Butler waited. He came galloping out to meet me, rope ladder swinging, with Irish Johnny already on his back.

"Cut him down."

I gripped the rungs and clambered aboard, joining Johnny in the howdah. "How're the kids?" I steadied myself on Butler's neck, taking up my rifle. Behind us, a mechanical lump waited on Butler's back—covered with a cloth. Waiting for the right time.

"Scared half out of their wits—but safe. They're in the professor's fancy wagon." Irish Johnny had a rope around his waist. "You getting on all right yourself, corporal?"

"Ah you know." I sent Butler lumbering out. "Just like the old days."

The Bracewell men had recovered from the fiery attack. That's when the guns started firing and when Butterscotch came out to play. Hewitt's scoped rifle cracked away from the rooftop, ripping a Bracewell detective right out of the saddle, leaving the horse to drag his body in the stirrups as it galloped crazily down the thoroughfare. One-Eyed Ginny and her gang unloaded their weapons from the windows of the abandoned saloon, splinters flying as their bullets tore into Elephant Head's other buildings and blasted Mulberry's men, who were trying in vain to find cover. Reeves came walking out of the old bank, firing his shotgun again and again and working the pump before tossing it aside and drawing his revolver for more.

And there was Butterscotch. She pounced on a screaming Bracewell detective, and his cry ended rapidly as those big sabers bit into his skull.

With death leaping all around, the Bracewell boys bunched up in the middle of the street. Just as we planned.

I stirred General Butler to a gallop. He came charging right at them, trumpeting madly. They saw it coming and raised their guns, but it was too late. We crashed right into them. Butler's tusks rushed down, a pair of ivory clubs, smashing into bone and leaving broken bodies on the sand. His trunk whipped down, encircling a horse and rider and hurling both into the wall of the general store. Butler's feet proved deadly themselves, kicking and stomping and leaving agony as he progressed.

Back in the day, when old Alexander the Great and Cleopatra had ridden out to battle on their war elephants, it must have been like this. Trampling feet. Screaming men, shattered by the enormity of what they faced.

But it wouldn't last for long.

"Make a stand, damn you!" Mulberry's voice. I spotted him, even if Prong was lost in the chaos.

He and the Bracewell gunmen had wisely abandoned their horses. They gathered on the boardwalk by the general store, taking what cover they could beside hitching posts and water troughs, and readied their repeating rifles. This was what we feared. The armored mastodon was still coming. If he and the infantry joined together, our surprise wouldn't bring victory. Already, a few shots snapped our way, more than a couple hitting Butler and making him snort and trumpet in pain.

I looked back at Johnny. "It's time?"

"Oh yeah." He scrambled back to the cloth. "Keep Butler steady. I'll do the rest."

The cloth fell away and there it was—the Gatling gun. A new model, specifically-designed to be fired from elephant-back. All gleaming brass and spinning barrels. Irish Johnny swiveled it toward the target and went to work.

His arm moved the crank in regular, even circles, his grip keeping it steady. The Gatling spun and spat out a storm of bullets. Each spin sent more lead burning through the air, making a set of loud pops that put me in the mind of an orchestra of rattlesnakes working their tails. I slowed Butler, forcing him to a walk even as the lead in his sides and legs made him want to run. Managed to look at where Johnny was shooting—to see the Gatling's result first hand.

Irish Johnny swept the front of the store and those bullets cut into the Bracewell men trying to find cover. He raked them with bullets. They danced back, splinters and chunks of blood and bone flying amongst them, shaking as the Gatling punched holes in guts and limbs and heads. Before the first body had even dropped into the dirt, Irish Johnny had sped to the next target. He kept the crank working the whole time, squinting while the Gatling breathed out carnage in that ghost town.

I'd heard of such weaponry, but this was the first time I'd seen them used on human targets. Lord Almighty—why should mankind ever fear the jaws of the saber-tooth tiger or the tusks of the mammoth? We are their superiors in slaughter, and we seem to make new and more terrible weapons with every passing day.

The Gatling fell silent. Johnny and I peered out, scanning the porch. "You see your man?" he asked.

"Mulberry? No—must've ducked inside." No sign of Prong either. That made me real nervous. But we had other troubles.

"Corporal Clarke!" It was Reeves. He had ducked for cover in an alley, threading new shells into his shotgun. "The mastodon's coming!"

And its cannon shot thundered, heralding its arrival. The blast missed us—but not by much. Struck the steeple in the old church instead, ripping the rusted bell right out of the tower. That bell came dancing down, bouncing and ringing all the while. As it stilled, the armored mastodon trundled closer, its crew already reloading.

If we let them take another shot, and they wouldn't need a third. Bullets could wound Butler. A cannonball would kill him.

"Any more ammunition for the Gatling?" I asked Johnny.

"Nah—too long to load it—and I don't know if it'd pierce the armor plating." His eyes flicked around, fear flashing in them for the first time. "We gotta run, Clarke."

"We do that and the mastodon will kill our friends." I patted General Butler's head. "We got one chance. Come on, old friend. One last charge."

I tightened my grip, bringing him to a charge once more. General Butler took one step and then another, upping his speed before breaking forward into a wild and free run—making straight for the mastodon. That pachyderm had armor, all right, but Butler was stronger and smarter and bigger. Would that decide the battle? I didn't know, but I held on tight as Butler gained speed. An elephant gallop—that always put a thrill in my heart. Now, we were riding straight for another elephant, and an ironclad one to boot. The mastodon's crew panicked, trying to reload the cannon before we reached them—before their mahout got the same idea and brought the mastodon to a charge as well.

Butler trumpeted. I screamed.

Then the beasts clashed. The world spun, the clatter of metal and flesh filling the world as choking dust rose. Mammoth feet slid and kicked as their trunks intertwined and wrestled. Butler slid to the side. Irish Johnny roared in Gaelic and his pistol flashed, blasting into the mastodon's crew as they tried to shoot back. The mastodon's tusk stabbed out, driving into Butler's shoulder. He had his trunk around the mastodon's throat, tugging it to the side. That armor—he couldn't pierce it. But it made the mastodon top heavy. Wouldn't take much to bring him down.

Unfortunately, Butler went down too. Gravity worked on us all.

We crashed into the side of the church. The wooden wall went. I slid from Butler's neck and the dancing dawn light twisted as splintery chunks and endless dust rained amongst us. Johnny screamed my name and then I took a tumble and gave the streets of Elephant Head a big fat kiss.

Getting up went slow. Molasses in the air, pressing against every limb. I managed to sit up and looked at the mastodon. It had been driven through the church, but light flickered in its eyes and it was rising too—right next to Butler. My mammoth bled from a nasty gash in the shoulder and lay on his side—trapped in the wreckage. No sign of Irish Johnny. No sign of much, thanks to the dust.

"Clarke!" One-Eyed Ginny's voice. She came dashing out, leveling that sawed-off shotgun of hers. She grabbed my shoulder, tugged me back, and the sawed-off thundered—just as the mastodon's trunk whipped out and struck her. Cast her aside—a toy tossed from a bored child—even as her shell punched into the mastodon's eye.

Now, I was on my feet. Wells—was she all right? And the mastodon. Poor critter. It didn't ask to be put into a tin can and set against me. Nobody here wanted any of this—apart from A.B. Mulberry and his men.

And Prong.

"Clement Clarke." That was his voice. Cutting through the haze of this nightmare dawn. I stumbled from the wreckage and there he was, right in the middle of the street with the sun burning above him. "Was hoping I'd get a chance to do this."

"Goddamn you…" I breathed out the words. I had my revolver on my hip and the howdah pistol under my vest, but they didn't matter much. Prong was faster. We both knew it.

"You see that?" Prong pointed behind us. I tried to see. More dust. "Colonel Custer's men. The Immortals. They'll be here soon—sweep away your little army of misfits and butcher the Indians. Just like Mr. Mulberry wanted. Not that I care much, I get paid no matter what happens." He shrugged. "But I'll be honest with you. What I do? I don't do it for the money."

"Corporal Clarke!" A young voice. Thalia.

My heart sank. She came running down the street—leaving her and young Maximilian's hiding place and rushing to my aid. Don't do it, darling. Stay hidden. Run away. Anything to get her from this monster who stood on the street before me.

"That ought to put some spring in your step." Prong nodded to her as she came rushing toward us. "Now let's get to it."

I drew—gritting my teeth and putting all my effort into clearing holster and firing at him. But as the pistol left leather, his revolver barked and my arm blazed. I buckled, dropping to my knees and clutching my arm. The pain welled up as my revolver tumbled into the dirt. White-hot burning, right behind my eyes. The only thing that hurt worse? Knowing what was coming next.

Prong walked closer to me. He stomped his boot on my pistol.

By then, Thalia had reached us—but she darted to the side, running to the fallen Butler instead. "General." Her fingers went through the fur on his head. "Please, General Butler, please—get up. Clarke needs you."

"Ain't that sad?" Prong asked. "Listening to her pleading?" He almost lazily aimed his pistol—right at my gut. "Why don't you plead too?"

I did. "Don't you—don't you hurt her." The begging crept weak from my mouth.

His thumb settled on the hammer of his Schofield. "Don't you worry." Then he spun it away. Aiming it at Thalia. "I'm gonna send her up to heaven before you."

"Butler!" Thalia hugged Butler's head, her arms not nearly reaching around his skull. "Please!"

And somewhere inside of him, that mammoth's heart pounded. With a love for me that nothing else can equal. But just as much love for her.

He sprang up. Rearing from the sundered church and making it to his feet. Snorting and shaking away the busted howdah—letting it tumble to the dust. Chunks of wood and streams of sand ran from him. Thalia leapt out of the way, falling on her belly. That saved her life, as Prong's pistol flashed. Shooting at Butler, though—not at her.

But it was a shot made out of panic. And it went wide.

Butler charged him. Prong brought up the gun again, his face split with terror—and then Butler's massive foot collided with his midsection. He went flying back, leaving the ground and flailing his arms before thudding hard into the dirt. A kick from a mammoth: you took that and you couldn't walk away. He lay there for just a moment, blood coursing from his gray lips, before the General took another step, posing his foot right above him, and stomped down.

That was the end of Orrin Prong.

Thalia ran to me. I tore my shirtsleeve free, tried to put a bandage around the wound. She knelt and helped me as One-Eyed Ginny limped over. All of us—General Butler included—were bloodied and weakened and on our last legs. Thalia alone was unharmed. And thank God for that. But she looked at the horizon. The dust cloud coming closer.

"It's Custer," she muttered. "And his killers."

"God." Wells spat in the dirt. "So after all that, we're still gonna get slaughtered? And there's still gonna be a war?"

Such seemed to be the prospects. The Immortals rode closer, a score of those scalp-hunting cavalrymen on galloping chargers. Custer himself rode at their head, on a fancy white horse. He even had his saber drawn, jabbing it into the air for dramatic effect more than anything else.

They were charging. Going straight for us, intending to trample and kill. And there wasn't much we could do about it.

Butler threw back his head and trumpeted. A long and defiant call, echoing over the plains.

I patted his leg. "It's all right, old friend. It's all right."

Another trumpet answered him. And another, and another still.

They came riding from the west of the town, cutting along the side of Elephant Head and galloping hard for the flank of the Immortals. A trio of war mammoths, with those special markings on their sides, along with horses and camels.

The envoy of the sovereign tribes. The masters of the plains.

They had seen us facing our doom and chosen to ride to our aid.

Running Eagle was with them, aiming a rifle from the back of her mammoth. I couldn't make out young Monty, but he was probably hiding out somewhere as well. Other Lakota warriors put arrows to their bows or aimed their rifles, readying their long war lances for what was to come. Peace meeting or not, they had come armed, and I removed my hat and watched as they crashed into the ranks of Custer's Immortals.

And proved that name false.

Right on the edge of Elephant Head, the battle raged. The Indian mammoths came first, crashing right in the center of the cavalry and parting the horses. Their arrows and rifle shots rained down as they rode through, and their own horsemen charged in to finish with swinging clubs and spears. The Immortals fought back, their guns roaring away, but they weren't ready to meet a charge from their flank.

The Lakota Nation were perhaps the finest Elephantry in the world and watching them work was something special. The Battle of Little Bigtusk must have been like this with the bloodshed magnified. I had walked away from the soldier's life a few years before of that battle and I was glad of it. Mighty glad.

"Oh no." Thalia gripped my good arm. "This is dreadful."

"What do you mean?" I waved to the Immortals. "Custer's boys were gonna kill us—now the Indians have saved our hides."

The white horse peeled away from the rest. Custer rode it hard, his sword abandoned. Clutching the reins, his bad leg jutting out—riding for all he was worth.

"But the Lakota have attacked American soldiers!" Thalia watched in horror. "General Crook shall demand a reprisal."

Wells watched grimly. "And they'll be war all over again." She spat on the ground. "Unless someone else takes the blame."

"What are you talking about?" I asked.

A trio of arrows whistled through the air and thudded in Custer's back. He drooped from the saddle and tumbled to the earth, coming to a halt not far from Thalia, Ginny, and myself. There, he lay, rolling over and gasping as his horse galloped into the distance with blood on its white flanks.

A tall Lakota swung down from mammoth-back on a rope and ran up to him. Dark fringed jacket, hair long—a stone warclub raised. Custer rolled over. "No!" He shouted, his voice hoarse. "Not you—Crazy Horse. Not—not again."

"You cannot dodge your destiny, *wasichu*." The club came hurtling down.

Crazy Horse claimed his kill and Custer's body lay dead in the dirt.

Thalia gasped and turned away. I had my good arm on her shoulder as footsteps came from behind us. Marshal Reeves and Lenora Hewitt, helping Irish Johnny along—he looked even worse than me. Matter of fact, nobody looked up for a turn around the ballroom. We were shot to hell, weakened, and staggering. Out of bullets and out of energy. Butterscotch padded along with them, ears perked up. They stood in the shadow of Butler as Crazy Horse, his club still stained with Custer's brains, walked closer. The other Lakota trailed after him.

We regarded each other. The seconds ticked by, as vultures wheeled up above and the flies began to buzz. A cold wind blew, whistling through the silent town. After a long time, Crazy Horse pointed his club at Butterscotch and spoke up. "That's a big cat."

"Hello there!" Young Carlos Montezuma poked his head out from the howdah of the she-mammoth as if a spell had been broken. He waved. "Are you all right?"

"You shouldn't have done that." I called to him and Crazy Horse and Running Eagle. "We came here to warn you—to stop you from killing American soldiers."

"They were about to fall upon you!" Monty cried. "We had—we had to save you."

"It'll be war now," I repeated. "With all the might of US government."

Crazy Horse didn't look particularly bothered. "It was always going to be war." He shook the blood from his club. "The boy thinks otherwise. He even convinced Sitting Bull, but I knew better. The *wasichu* do not care about the costs, in their dead or our dead. They want war and we will have to meet them. So let us welcome battle. Let Iya's Children ride, one last time." His eyes blazed. "We will die for the Black Hills. *Hoka hey.*"

I didn't have the strength to argue with him. And why not? He was right. "Wait. I got a plan." Wells snapped her fingers, her boots tapping on the dust. "But I'll need your help. We gotta get my pet dancing sloth out here, put his claws to work." She removed her eye-patch, tearing it free. "And we've got to make sure there ain't no witnesses."

Her plan involved that dancing sloth, Pierrot? It didn't make much sense. As for witnesses, we'd killed all the Bracewell detectives, and the Indians were finishing off Custer's boys. The only one I hadn't seen die is—Lady came galloping out, whickering madly. It sounded for all the world like a warning—or a cry of panic. Thalia knelt down and caught the horse. She seemed just as terrified.

Then a scream came further up the street in Elephant Head, and a terrified, shrill trumpet too. Professor Ashe's Ambulatory Arcanum came rattling down, Professor Ashe staggering out of it—a blood coursing from his chest. A.B. Mulberry was at the reins of the painted wagon, cracking them madly—a revolver shoved into Maximilian's cheek. The boy sat next him on the coachman's seat, trying to get to his uncle as they rode along.

"Max!" Thalia called for him and ran out. I grabbed her shoulder and wrenched her back—stopping her from going under the wheels.

That colorful wagon rode for the horizon, bearing Mulberry and his little hostage with it.

Mulberry would be the witness. Spinning a tale of American soldiers butchered by the Braves of the Indian Nations. He'd have the whole of the country spoiling for a fight.

"We've got to go after him!" Thalia cried.

Crazy Horse watched them go. "Our mammoths still battle on. Yours doesn't look fit to ride."

"And I'm hurt worse. Same with the rest of us." I looked at General Butler and patted my arm. "Thalia, darling—I don't think…"

"I'll ride the General." Her eyes gleamed. Rufus Ridgeway had gotten that expression, right before he did something crazy. "Come with me, corporal. You get on the back and I'll ride him—right after the man who ordered my father killed. I've practiced it and you'll be there to guide me." She patted my side and walked toward Butler. "Now come along. Today, we ride for justice."

I looked at Butler and then at the others. Irish Johnny grinned. "Best do as she says, boy-o."

Smug bastard. I patted his shoulder and limped to Butler, who had already knelt down. Thalia scrambled onto his back and took up a position on the neck—the mahout's position.

She was her father's daughter. She knew how to ride.

We set Butler at a good canter after the Ambulatory Arcanum. I settled on Butler's back while Thalia directed him. Since the howdah fell off, I had nothing but the General's skin and bristly hair to keep me in place. Still, there was plenty of it and I wouldn't be tumbling off anytime soon. Even though his gait had a roll in it, a limp from the wound he'd taken off that mastodon. Blood went down his leg, leaving a trail behind him, just as blood soaked my own makeshift bandage.

Neither of us was in good shape.

"You don't got to lead him so much." I gave Thalia the instruction as we went down the road, cresting the hill. "Keep your grip loose. He knows what he's doing. You just got to stay out of his way some."

She swallowed and looked back. "But I'm doing all right?"

Don't let the darkness take you. Not yet. You still had to kill Mulberry. Save that poor peddler's boy and protect Thalia. "You're doing fine, darling." I swallowed. "You'd make your daddy proud."

Her eyes shone.

A bullet cracked in the air. Mulberry. He had brought the Ambulatory Arcanum to the cluster of wagons where his goons had made camp. It was empty now, though a pair of camels waited at his fancy carriage and the Short-Faced Bear roared in its cage.

Mulberry had hopped down from the wagon, dragging Maximilian with him. He shoved him toward the carriage and cracked off another shot—but he was no pistolero. Couldn't even hit Butler with it. I drew with my left and fired again—making him keep his head down. Thalia cried out at every shot. I sent a few burning out. No chance of hitting anything. Unlike Wild Bill, I could only fire with my right. But at least it kept his head down.

And I still had the howdah pistol, with its two shots. For that one, I'd have to fire up close. So that even with my left I couldn't miss.

"Don't come any closer!" Mulberry cried. The bear echoed his voice with a roar. "I'll kill the boy! I swear to God, I will put a bullet in his brain!"

Thalia looked at me, terrified. "What do I do?"

"Charge." I swallowed. "Knock down the carriage. Then I'll get off, you get Max and I'll kill Mulberry." I pointed to her. "Tighten your legs a little. Give Butler's head a pat. He'll do the rest." Whiteness flashed in my eyes. Not yet—damn it. Not yet.

"Come on, then, General." She whispered to Butler. "Please."

And he did it. Charged up the hill. I gripped mammoth fur and bounced up and down, each movement making my wound hurt worse. My eyes closed for a little and then I forced them open. We were on them, reaching Mulberry's carriage. Butler brought his head down and shoved it aside, the two camels making their panicked bellows as they dragged it away. Mulberry and Maximilian both went sprawling.

I clambered to the edge of Butler. "Put her down, General!" I called to him as I shimmied, fearing the drop. "Gently now!" Then I let go.

Hard earth caught my fall. I rolled into it avoiding too much damage, and made it to my feet. Mulberry lay across from me, on his back—Maximillian sprawling next to him. He had his pistol up and aimed at me. The boy grabbed at him, receiving a wallop for the trouble as the revolver barked.

Drove a bullet straight into my leg.

I dropped down, rolling over. Pain washed over, something slick filling my trousers. Mulberry aimed again—and his revolver clicked on an empty chamber.

I drew the howdah pistol and took a limping sort of jump at him. Made it to his waist.

We crashed down together and rolled.

"Run, Max!" I shouted to the kid as Mulberry forced my arm to the earth. Reflex made me pull the trigger and the shot thundered—kicking up dust and deafening me.

Then Mulberry was on top of me, pushing me back—slamming my head into the bars of the bear cage. Its roars came from far away—the world echoing thanks to the howdah pistol's first shot. Bear spittle settled on the tip of my ear. Mulberry had his pen knife out, pushing my pistol back as he drove that wicked little tooth into my belly and chest. Little cuts, but they'd add up.

I wedged the howdah pistol up. Jabbing it under his chin.

He gripped my arm with both hands and twisted it. I fought back, pointing it up. Aiming at the lump of metal dangling above us. Then I pulled the trigger.

Another roar. Another profusion of black powder. Something clanked and rattled and came free as I dropped the howdah pistol completely.

Mulberry leaned back. He'd taken some hits too—his nose bloodied, his fancy suit tattered and covered in dust, his hair wild. "Missed!" He sneered as he turned the word into an insult. "One shot left in that double-barreled gun and you missed!" He gripped my throat. What strength I had left failed me. Wasn't much I could do to stop him.

But smile.

"Didn't…" I got the word out and looked up.

The lock on the door of the bear cage. My howdah pistol had shattered it.

The lock tumbled away as the Short-Faced Bear slammed against it and burst out into the clear air.

A dark comet of a paw crashed into Mulberry. Lifting him off his feet and slamming him to the earth. I hit the floor and rolled, then started crawling away toward Butler, who was trumpeting madly. Roars behind me. Mulberry had started to scream. Short-Faced Bears don't waste much time when they've got prey and he was going through Mulberry with gusto. Caging that bear hadn't done nothing to make it less wild

I crawled away from the carnage as Mulberry's screams faded. Then I sank down, getting a better look at the dirt. "Clarke!" Thalia's hand on mine. She got my arm over her shoulder and helped me up.

"Is he okay? Is he all r-right?" Maximilian's voice. He was up on General Butler's back, the blue sky above him.

"Fine." Thalia managed.

"Goliath!" Maximilian cried. "We need to get Goliath!"

A moment like this and he thought about the pygmy mammoth. Well, that was all right. He was a kid. They always loved their pets.

"Go and get the boy's little elephant," I whispered to Thalia. "Butler will help me."

She winced and gently let me down at Butler's feet, then scrambled off. I rolled over a little and watched her skirt the Short-Faced Bear, who was snacking on what was left of Mulberry, and reach the Ambulatory Arcanum. She worked at the reins, freeing Goliath. The pygmy mammoth trumpeted and stomped his feet, but she'd manage him. Get him—and the rest of us—out of there before the Short-Faced Bear was done with Mulberry.

Something soft encircled my waist. I left the earth, but it was no angel who carried me aloft. My arms hung limp and I caught a glimpse of General Butler's face as I went up. Had a look at him. Wrinkled and old and tired, covered in dust and scars old and new. He was a tired old beast.

But his eyes. There's something about a mammoth's eyes.

They're big as pie plates and have an amber glow to them. Pure gold and flecked with shadow. You can get lost, looking into a mammoth's eyes. Seeing them takes you back to a time when man called the caves home. It teaches you that for all our killing power and intelligence, we're not too far off from those times. We're not the biggest thing in the world. Not even close.

Butler's eyes told me all that, and something else as well. They told me that he was my friend. I was honored to share that.

General Butler hefted me up and set me on his back. I lay there, bleeding from my arm and my leg and my chest and looked up at the sky. Pure blue, streaked with fluffy clouds. Still with the cold of the prairie, but with enough sunlight to match. It was going to be a beautiful day.

Maximilian's face appeared, looking down at me. "Mr. Clarke—oh God—my uncle—and you—are you going to die?" His freckled cheeks bore a bad bruise and tears streaked them. Poor guy. I wasn't much older than him when I lost my father.

"It'll be…all right." I smiled at him. "Thalia…she'll take you back to your uncle…"

And One-Eyed Ginny Wells, with her wild plan to save the day. Whatever that was.

Another snort from Butler. The trunk came up again, this time bearing Thalia. More of the squeaky, little trumpeting from Goliath. He was at Butler's side. "Don't worry." Thalia's voice. Her face loomed above me, next to Maximilian. "Goliath's fine. He'll go with us. Back to town."

"Thank you." Maximilian was crying openly now.

Thalia too. The tears came thick and fast. Staying hidden from the chaos of the battle, racing out to see General Butler lying down and me getting shot by Prong, and then this wild ride out here to save the boy—not to mention seeing a guy get eaten by a bear—and finally getting revenge for her father—all of that had to be boiling up inside of her.

Now, she could let it out.

I got my good arm up and patted her shoulder. "Don't cry, darling." I gave her my best smile.

Then the darkness reached up and pulled me down.

CHAPTER EIGHT

RIDE INTO THE SETTING SUN

It was bad dreams mixed with worse moments of consciousness for me, until full wakefulness came stealing up. My eyes flickered open. Harsh light made me wish I kept them closed. Scratchy army blankets against my bare toes. Prairie cold playing on my face tempered a mite by the blaze in the hearth. I gave my cheek a touch. More stubble than I cared to have—and there was a bandage on that arm too, thick around the elbow. Another on my leg, and more on my belly.

"So you're awake." Colonel MacDougal's voice. I rolled over. He sat next to my bed, one of a row of the same, set on dusty floorboards. Probably Fort Fielding's infirmary. "And well that you are." Next to him, Thalia slumbered, with Lady curled up next to her. "We feared for you, Corporal Clarke. None more than she."

I managed to sit up. The world went for a spin and MacDougal pressed a canteen to my lips. I drank an ocean to coat my dry throat and looked down at my wounds. "It's not that bad. I've been hurt worse than this." Though I couldn't recall when. My eyes went to Thalia. "How's she keeping?"

"Oh, well enough. I've brought her food from the canteen, and the others have been looking in on her. She's stayed by your side, Clarke." He smiled sadly.

"Don't wake her yet." I pulled back the blanket. I was only dressed in my union suit, and MacDougal had stashed some new garments—my old ones were doubtlessly covered in blood—next to me. I slid into some jeans and worked the buttons on my shirt, before reaching for a vest. My gun belt and weaponry—that remained as well. "MacDougal." I hesitated, but then went ahead. "What happened out there?"

"The damnedest thing, Corporal." He put on an expression of false confusion. "It seems that the Indians and Custer's worthies weren't the only ones riding around out there."

"Oh yeah?"

"Some eastern tycoon was apparently on a hunting expedition. Brought along a small army of Bracewell Detective gunmen for company." He shrugged. "They all met their end out there."

Now, I forced falseness into my voice. "However did that happen?"

"Short-Faced Bear, apparently. Went on a rampage and killed them all." He shrugged. "And that's not even the strangest thing that happened."

"What do you mean?"

"Well, Custer and his soldiers arrived at the scene, and were massacred. A gang of outlaws are the culprits, led by the notorious One-Eyed Ginny Wells." Now, the false confusion mixed with the real. "They ambushed him with some sort of killer sloth—Colonel Allensworth's Longhorn Soldiers found the remains of Custer and his men scattered over the hill, with claw marks in their bodies. One-Eyed Ginny's eye-patch as well. Add that to some eyewitness testimony from the Indians, and we know who is responsible for Custer's demise."

Ginny Wells—she was supremely clever. A whole cavalry company—that would earn her respect in outlaw circles. Well, if Reverend Allensworth hadn't decided to keep her secret, it wouldn't hold. I guess I had both of them to thank.

"What about the Indians?"

"They stopped by in the fort for a while—diplomatic guests—and the territorial governor invited them in to meet with him. From there, I believe that they intend to proceed to Washington to meet with the president."

"So the treaty will hold?"

MacDougal shrugged. "For now. There will perhaps be incursions and future conflicts—and future wars—but the treaties will hold. For now."

I threaded my belt through its hole and tightened it. My various wounds still ached, but now that I was dressed and back on my feet, I felt a little more like myself. What sort of carnage had been averted by all the bloodshed in Elephant Head? A greater war in the Black Hills? Crazy Horse, Sitting Bull, and the rest had done that—by winning, by standing strong, and kept their nation alive. Maybe now, Washington D.C., the railroad interests, the gold-hungry prospectors and settlers and the like would learn to leave well enough alone.

And what would happen, a hundred years hence? The same sort of thing? An association of sovereign tribes, free to manage their own affairs, in the middle of the United States? Locked in an uneasy peace with their surroundings? The

Canadians had that, with the *Syndicat Metis*, and even England had learned to live with Gran-Haiti taking over a good portion of Jamaica and adding that to its holdings in the Caribbean, along with the Free City of New Orleans.

It could have gone differently. It could have gone worse. If that gunfight had played out differently, if Crazy Horse and young Monty had ridden in just a little later, we'd have been finished. Or what if the US Cavalry had been luckier during the war of '76 and crushed the Lakota after the Little Bigtusk? And what if Abraham Lincoln's pet sloth hadn't gone with him to Ford's Theatre and Booth had gunned him down, like those assassins who killed poor Seward and Johnson? There might not be the Freedman's Towns. Little things—like the great animals not being there—could create a history where greed, violence, and hatred won out, again and again. What kind of nightmare world would that be?

It boggled the mind.

"I'm gonna take the air, Mortimer," I said.

"Go on," MacDougal agreed. "We ought to let Miss Ridgeway sleep a little more. She was up half the night waiting for the doctors to do their business and standing guard. And she weren't the only one." He waved the door. "He's out there."

I knew who he meant.

Outside the infirmary, General Butler waited. The day had come cold, little flecks of snow drifting down from a greying sky. His sort of weather. As soon as I emerged, his trunk came snaking down and wrapped around me. I hugged it back and looked into his eyes. The docs had helped him too—stitching up his various wounds and keeping him well-fed and watered. He was old, yes, but still strong.

A world without General Butler. A world without mammoths. That wasn't the kind of world I wanted to live in.

"Easy there, General." I worked my fingers through the fur on his trunk and patted his forehead as he leaned down. "I'm here."

He made some happy snuffling noises and then pulled back his trunk and trumpeted for all the world to hear.

"Yeah, she's here too. Don't you worry." I reached up and scratched him below the chin, enough to make his trunk wiggle with joy.

"Corporal." A familiar voice—the Reverend Colonel Allensworth. He must have just returned from a ride, and led his charger across the fort's courtyard. "Good to see you up and about." He handed the reins of his horse to a stableboy and ambled over, the wind stirring his blue greatcoat. "You took some hits. Trading bullets with that outlaw gang, no doubt."

"Yeah," I agreed—the lie thick in my words. "A bunch of outlaws and a giant

…and patted his foreheac

killer sloth butchering Custer and a column of US Cavalry. Who could've thought of such a thing?"

"Who indeed?" Allensworth arched an eyebrow. Oh yes. He knew the truth. "I do have another question—what do you intend to do with that young lady in there?"

My fingers froze on Butler's furred neck. "I never really considered it. Maybe take her back to her grandparents." But even as I said that, I knew I couldn't do it. They hated her. It would be a hard life for Thalia if I did that. "There's no alternative. I can't look after her. Can't raise her myself."

The reverend shrugged. "Are you so certain? What have you been doing for these past weeks, Corporal Clarke?"

Looking after her. Raising her.

"Well, I'm a bounty hunter. I travel around, seeking outlaws—what sort of life is that for a child?"

"Perhaps it needn't be your lot forever." Allensworth looked at the door to the infirmary. "But such things are merely details. I have seen numerous families, of all kinds, during my years on this earth, and there is but one measure which leads to their success: care. You care for her, Corporal Clarke. So what else is there to say?"

"Learn that in the bible, reverend?"

A low laugh from Allensworth. "The Lord walked the earth, did he not? And so it is earthly matters that I've concerned myself with. The same goes for you. Now, go and greet young Miss Ridgeway, and keep what I said in mind."

General Butler snorted again and I patted him as I started back toward the infirmary. "All right. I'll go and get her."

I pushed open the door and walked in—and Thalia came running down the planks and threw herself into my arms. I hugged her back. Care—oh yes. We had plenty of that.

When she let go, she brushed tears from her eyes on her sleeve. "You're well."

"Well enough," I agreed. "To ride, I suppose. And to travel."

"That's grand," she agreed.

I stood beside her, motioning to the door—and General Butler out there. "Would you like to ride with me, for a spell?"

She nodded. "For a spell." Hesitant—as if not wishing to ruin what I'd established. "That would be very nice."

"All right. I'll need to get a new howdah and some supplies, and then we'll light out. I'll give you some money, you go to the fort store and pick up some treats for the road. Something for me, something for you, and something for the General—you know what he likes."

"Very well." She said it casually—after all, we'd done this sort of thing before.

"And where will we go?"

"West," I said. "How's that sound?"

She slipped into a Western drawl. "Mighty fine."

I chuckled and then we went to get ready for our journey.

The sun had come up and shined bright and cold. Put a gleam on the frost of the prairie and sent snowflakes dancing down from the heavens. General Butler liked this sort of weather and I didn't mind it much—especially with a buffalo robe and some scarves, straight from Fort Fielding's store. Thalia took the mahout's seat and I got to rest on the howdah, snacking on a ham sandwich and a pickle, washed down with coffee.

It was a nice road to travel.

We come to a crossroads, where two other travelers waited. I sat up as General Butler snorted and swung his trunk down. Little Goliath—pulling a battered buckboard instead of the painted Ambulatory Arcanum—reached his miniature trunk for a one-sided mammoth handshake. Professor Ashe and Maximilian sat on the buckboard, bundled up for the cold as well. Behind them, Marshal Reeves rode on his mare. Lenora Hewitt and Irish Johnny shared another wagon, this one well-covered—probably because Butterscotch sat inside. The big cat poked his head out and gave us a look that was equal parts quizzical and hungry.

I touched the brim of my hat. "Howdy."

"Greetings, my good man! Greetings!" Ashe doffed his fez while Max waved excitedly. "Thalia Ridgeway—I owe you my nephew's life." He patted his chest. "And I owe Marshal Reeves my own. He stopped my bleeding and carried me back to the doctors of Fort Fielding."

"Funny, how things work out," Reeves agreed.

"Where you bound now?" I asked—keeping one eye on Butterscotch. "All of you?"

"Johnny and I are going to his cabin," Hewitt said. "Pick up a few things. Then we're heading south. More Freedman's Towns need defending."

"And I suppose I'm not done soldiering," Johnny added. "Besides, I have a feeling they'll be many fine sales to be made down south, and I'll need a market for my weapons if the treaties hold and peace reigns on the prairies."

"I suppose we did sort of ruin your business," Thalia muttered.

"Ah, think nothing of it," Johnny said. "There's war in Mexico, you know. Juarez against the Emperor and his French masters. Plenty of opportunities to be found down there." He reached back, resting his palm on Butterscotch's fuzzy forehead. That was Irish Johnny all right—pure fearlessness. "Maybe Miss Hewitt will go with me. Play the part of the gun-for-hire. It was good to rekindle our friendship, so I have you to thank for that."

"And I, sir, must thank you for turning me away from the sinner's path." Professor Ashe put a solemn expression on his face. "I now find myself not only in the law's good graces but in their service." But beyond the brag, he didn't seem particularly happy. "Not that I have a choice in the matter."

"We've struck a bargain," Reeves said. "I'll make use of them, back in Fort Smith. There's plenty of outlaw gangs who'll run when I come riding up, but will let a harmless snake oil salesmen talk his way into their good graces." He nodded toward Ashe. "The professor here's gonna be my spy."

"We're gonna be deputized," Maximilian said happily.

"You will not be deputized." But a little gentleness crept into his voice as he looked them over. "But I'll look after you. And I'll make sure the boy's all right."

From one danger to another—that was the professor's life now. "Well, you take care—and you've always got a friend on a mammoth who can help you." I looked ahead.

The road split—one branch going south, one going east, and one going west. One road for the each of us. I went a little taller, looking down at this wild collection who had become my friends. Circumstance had thrown us together, more or less. Irish Johnny was a friend from the war, but coincidence and bad luck had put me on the same trail as Hewitt, the Ashes, and the Marshal.

And yet, they'd stood by me. Fought with me, bled with me. Together, we'd won.

"I ain't got—I ain't got the words to thank you."

"Please," Thalia added. "Accept our deepest gratitude."

"Hell, Thalia," Johnny replied. "We know that."

Then we parted ways. Hewitt and Irish Johnny rode south. The professor, young Maximilian, and Marshal Reeves went east. And Thalia and I headed west.

After a good day's riding, we came to a ramshackle frontier trading post. Didn't offer much—a structure of sod and planks, with a Longhorn Buffalo skull mounted above the door. Nearby, an oddity. Some old trees stood, overlooking a half-frozen creek. They still had some green on them. Right now, a giant ground sloth was working on the leaves, using his heavy claws to pull the branches down and his tongue to dine on the leaves. Not just any sloth. He had a little tattered vest, and a conical hat.

No doubt about it—this was Pierrot.

"Corporal—" Thalia started.

"I see him. You go and let Butler get a snack. I'll go and have a look."

I left the General to his meal with Thalia to watch him. Then I forced open the door and slid inside, letting the lantern light wash on me, and looked at scuffed tables where a few other travelers drank rotgut to keep them warm on the trail.

Sure enough, One-Eyed Ginny was one of them. She sat with a newspaper, looking it over through her good eye—a new strip of cloth forming a temporary patch. Some of her gang lounged around as well, all watching as I approached her.

"I didn't know you could read," I said.

She lowered the newspaper. "I got one eye but it works just fine. I take a look at you, though, and wish it didn't." She set down the paper and pointed to the headline. "You had a look at this, Clarke?"

Wild Bill Hickock—A Legend Meets His End.

I eyeballed the story. The writer got bits and pieces right, but not the particulars. Wild Bill Hickock had gone to battle against a dozen guns and killed his fair share of them before dying himself. It was a blaze of glory, and one that would stand forever in the annals of the west.

Wells leaned back. "So that's his end, huh?"

"Yeah. The one he chose."

"Few of us get to do that. Me? I'm gonna try and make it to Mexico. Might be the only safe place, now that I'm the notorious killer of Custer."

"Thank you, for that."

She snorted. "Ah, think nothing of it. Adds to my rep, I'd say. Big time." She peered out the doorway. "That Thalia with you?"

"Yes, ma'am. I'm looking after her, I suppose."

"Good." She motioned to the newspaper. "Wild Bill's end—it's a good one. They'll be writing dime novels about it for centuries. The Last Stand of Wild Bill. Matter of fact, sometimes I wonder if I wouldn't like something like that. Or if a Last Stand is the best I can hope for. But you, Clement Clarke, you deserve something else." She nodded to the doorway. "She's out there, riding that mammoth. You take care of her, Clarke."

"I intend to," I said, and meant it.

I went to the wall, where an old noticeboard waited. Who had ivory to sell, who was looking for a trail boss to lead a wagon train out west—and a few Wanted posters. I found a likely one—William H. Bonney, riding under the alias of Billy the Kid. He was wanted for rustling and murder, but didn't look old enough to shave. Running him down and hauling him in would be easy as fetching eggs from a henhouse. I tore the poster from the board and rolled it up.

Touched my hat to Wells. "I'll be seeing you around, Ginny."

"Count on it," she agreed. "Happy trails, Clarke."

"Same to you."

Back outside, Butler had given Pierrot a friendly nudge—pushing the big sloth away from the tree so he could get his fill. Thalia sighed and gave him a talking-to for his rudeness, then reached up, snapped off a branch laden with leaves, and tossed it to Pierrot. She lowered the rope ladder as I ambled over.

"What now, Corporal?"

I showed her Billy the Kid's poster. "He's down New Mexico way, but is rumored to be heading north. Let's get him."

"Let's," she agreed, and gave Butler's head a pat. He started to trot his way back to the road.

I settled back on the howdah. Thalia was a natural—born to the mahout's position. The General was pleased to have her atop him. I shouldn't have been surprised—she was Rufus Ridgeway's girl, after all.

Up above, the sun started to dip—going down early this time of year. That orange haze dripped low, in the direction of our journey. We rode on. For the first time in a long time, I felt good about what waited beyond the next sunset.

THE END

Special Preview Book Two:

BEHEMOTH

CHAPTER ONE

Congress of Rough Riders

There's nothing like an elephant to make a circus memorable. Of course, my mount, General Butler, was far from an ordinary elephant. He was a mammoth—a Columbian Mammoth. The King of Plains, and a veteran of the Civil War as well. Most folks who went to the circus didn't expect to see a war mammoth come strutting out.

Of course, Buffalo Bill's Wild West Show was pretty far from your ordinary circus.

I sat on top of General Butler in the wings of some big old amphitheater, waiting for our cue. Both of us were dressed for the occasion.

"I feel ridiculous," I muttered.

I certainly looked the part, with a fringed buckskin jacket and trousers draped in shimmering spangles—all snow-white. I had a white Stetson to match, and a pair of pearl-handled revolvers polished to a brilliant shine and loaded with blanks. Below me, General Butler had a sparkly bridle and little golden orbs set on the tips of his tusks. His fur had been oiled and combed. They'd done everything but put bows on him.

"You look splendid." Thalia Ridgeway sat on the howdah, a Winchester repeater—also loaded with blanks—across her knees. My adopted daughter. Just turned twelve. Of course, having a Chinese girl riding on mammoth back wouldn't really fit into the story Buffalo Bill had wanted to tell with me, so she'd gotten a costume of her own: a Norfolk jacket and tie and a cowboy hat with feathers in the hat band.

Now, she was Tulsa Tom Thompkins, my loyal sidekick.

Ain't show business grand?

I sighed. "Soon as this is over, me and Cody will have words."

"Words of gratitude, I hope—for all the good he's done us." Thalia straightened. "Oh—it's time. Remember, corporal—smile."

I forced a smile on my lips and set General Butler to trot on out. We rode him right into the middle of the amphitheater, to booming applause and the accompanying prairie orchestra's swelling sounds. Buffalo Bill Cody himself stood on a little stage facing the stands, hoisting up a speaking trumpet to address the crowd as Butler trotted out.

"There he is, folks—Corporal Clement Clarke—the Peerless Pistolero and Matchless Manhunter of the Wild West!" Cody had on showman's finery, a tan fringed jacket embroidered with swirling floral designs, his golden hair falling down his shoulders in a magnificent mane.

Brilliant electric lights gleamed on his stage, more flashing on us. I couldn't make out the audience, but from what I'd heard, the denizens of Chicago had filled the arena to capacity. That storm of applause certainly proved good numbers. I forced my hand up in a wave and didn't forget to smile. General Butler arched his trunk and trumpeted and Thalia waved as well. We passed the stage, just like we had practiced.

Cody kept up the patter as neared the pantomime structures in the center. "Yes, Clement Clarke—soldier, scout, bounty hunter. A boyhood on the Kansas Plains, part of it spent in the company of the infamous John Brown himself! Then, a brilliant career in the fire and steel of the Vicksburg Campaign, in which he led the 2nd Elephantine Dragoons to victory. I don't have to tell you what he rode in those battles, folks—take a look yourselves! That's General Butler—the pride of the plains! Countless pounds of all-American war mammoth. Ain't he pretty, folks?"

Butler trumpeted again and shook his ears.

"Hogging the glory." I patted his head fondly.

"Corporal!" Thalia hissed to me. "Bring him to the cabin!"

Right—the cabin. It lay just up ahead, a little construction of plywood set amongst potted sagebrush. I directed Butler toward the cabin and drew one of my pistols. I gave it a little spin, making it blur about, before aiming it at the cabin.

"Come on out, evil-doer!" I shouted. "And face justice!" I glanced back at Thalia.

She gave me an encouraging nod. I appreciated it—but acting wasn't my strong suit. Some of the performing capybaras that went on before us could probably have done a better job.

More narration from Cody. "For these past years, Clarke has pursued all manner of horrible outlaws. His trade is that of the bounty hunter—or bounty killer, as the case may be. What you're about to witness, my friends, is something that Clarke's done almost every day out in the lawless frontier. Witness the hideout of the notorious desperado, Raven Ramon!"

Raven Ramon popped out, right as his name was said. He wore a black duster, black shirt, and black hat—with ebony on his pistols. He'd even grown a massive black moustache for the part. Hisses and boos resounded from the audience.

Raven Ramon—El Cuervo, they'd called him—had once worked the border country as an actual outlaw. Cody, you see, always sought verisimilitude. I guess Ramon preferred having jeers thrown at him instead of bullets.

Still, his acting skills weren't much better than mine. He pointed at me and glowered. "You dare try and bring me to justice? Take not one step closer, bounty hunter, or you will imperil the life of my innocent hostage!" He waved to the door.

A petite woman entered, clad in an ochre dress and cowboy hat, her brown hair in a tumble of curls. "Corporal Clarke—don't listen to him!" Gasps from the audience. Putting a pretty hostage into the action always got the audience interested.

It was Thalia's line. She stood tall on the howdah. "We'll save you, little missy—if my name ain't Tulsa Tom Thompkins!" Her squeaky voice got some laughter, and her face reddened as she smiled.

Next up was Raven Ramon. "You won't succeed, Corporal Clarke—not against my flock of evil!" No response. This wasn't right. He raised his voice, turning around on the porch. "Not against my flock of evil!"

The flock of evil arrived—and it still wasn't right. Three oversized birds—but these weren't the kind you'd see eating crumbs at the park. Each stood as tall as a man on long, lean legs tipped with nasty claws. Arched necks supported oversized yellow beaks, nasty chompers that could rend flesh and break bone. Colorful feathers shone in the lights—one sky blue and green, the other glossy black, and the third brilliant crimson. Terror Birds. That's what they called them. They couldn't fly, and that was a mercy.

But they should've been leashed—and they weren't. Something had gone wrong and now those birds were coming straight for us.

"Clarke?" Thalia asked. The Terror Birds advanced on Ramon and his hostage, snapping their beaks in anticipation of an easy meal.

I aimed my pistol at the first bird and fired. It cracked and boomed—only firing a blank. That wasn't going to work.

Cody was waving to the roustabouts, keeping up his speech to the audience. Convincing them nothing was wrong. Ramon had his own pistols out and stood in front of his prisoner, but his had blanks too. There was one thing I could do to help.

I tightened my knees. Stirred the General to a gallop.

He came charging in, lowering his head. The red bird spun around and took a leap at him—and caught a tusk. Butler was smart. He knew he had the size, if not the speed, to beat these overgrown turkeys down. The crimson Terror Bird dropped in a heap, feathers flying, and the blue one took a nasty leap for his face—which was just what General Butler wanted. His trunk lashed out, caught the bird by its big neck, and rocked it up and down. Made the wattle dance. Then he sent it flying back and crashing next to its red buddy.

The black bird went for a flank. The squawking came from the side and he was up on Butler's side, his claws tearing into the fancy blanket as his beak snapped at Thalia. My heart pounded. That girl—I was looking after her. I'd only signed on with the Wild West Show because I figured it would be safer for her.

Thalia spun her repeater around. Didn't bother shooting. Instead, she swung the gun and clubbed the fancy, studded butt into the Terror Bird's beak. Sent it tumbling down from Butler and to the ground. It scampered back to its fellows.

All three stood together, squawking and snapping their beaks and ready for another attack. They could dart around Butler, pecking at him and drawing blood—weakening him before going for the throat. Or go for me. Or Thalia.

"Hey, birds!" The hostage stood up. She held out her hand and one of the roustabouts tossed her the rifle. "Your goose is cooked."

The rifle fired. It blasted across the amphitheater. She didn't hit any of the birds, but she wasn't aiming at them. Because this woman was Annie Oakley and she never missed.

Sure enough, an engine came humming to life. A deep rumbling hit the air and sand went in crazy spirals. The giant motorized fan—a new purchase for Cody—that had been waiting in a little tent at the edge of the field. Oakley's bullet had turned it on. That fan was supposed to be for the finale of the show—the great tornado that would tear this settler's cabin to pieces and send a bunch of performers, trained camels, horses, and even an albino pygmy mammoth named Li'l Snowball running for cover.

Now, the wind struck the Terror Birds. Feathers flew. They went down, smashing into each other like ninepins. The scarlet bird even lifted up the air a little and got to enjoy flying before ramming into the side of the cabin.

By then, someone switched off the fan. The Terror Bird keepers, all looking apologetic, came rushing out with leashes and muzzles and dragged the birds away.

The audience watched it all.

I swallowed and removed my hat. One thing Cody had told me stuck in my mind: the show must go on. "Ladies and gentlemen, Annie Oakley!" I waved the hat to Oakley, who made a polite curtsy.

Great applause from everyone. Raven Ramon bowed and Thalia and I did as well. Butler dipped his head too—and that got plenty of applause. On the stage, Cody gave me a knowing, thankful nod—and Annie Oakley gave me a wink.

That evening, Thalia and I joined the other performers in Buffalo Bill Cody's tent. This had been the first show and he had the cooks make something nice for the occasion: prime ribs cooked up Texas-style, with baked potatoes and roasted corn as well. Thalia and I filled our plates and settled down with the others.

Cody hoisted his glass to me. "Well, hello there, Clement. I have to thank you—your mammoth held those birds at bay. Hell, he nearly stole the show."

"That's all Butler, Cody." I worked on the ribs while Thalia carefully put a napkin in her collar. "How was the take?"

"Oh, very good, very good. Great start to the season."

"The season?" I asked. "How many more shows?"

He laughed. "Come on, Clement. We just started."

Raven Ramon sat next to me. He passed me the wine bottle. "Cheer up. We get a good hotel in this town—unlike many others—and the audience doesn't want to throw anything at me or insist on getting involved in the action. And none of our animals tried to eat any of them."

"It's better than soldiering, at least," Cody said. "Or scouting."

"You got me there," I agreed.

Thalia had been listening carefully. "That's where you met? In the war?"

"Correct," Cody said. "Though it wasn't the proper Civil War, like you learned in school. Armies of blue and gray marching back and forth and exchanging rifle and cannon fire and the like." A distant look appeared in his eyes. Maybe it had been a long time since Cody thought about his Kansas boyhood.

I tried not to think on it often.

"A more personal kind of war. Jayhawkers and Border Ruffians. You'd know who you were riding after. Go to their farm and surprise them. Burn it down and then ride away—dodging revolver rounds as you ran through the woods."

I looked at the plate. "And what they did—the Rebels—the kind of bloodshed they unleashed—" I stopped myself. "It ain't fitting conversation for a pleasant dinner."

We resumed eating and some better words came to replace the sad ones.

Then Annie Oakley poked her head in. "Hey, Mr. Mammoth Rider." She waved to me. "There's a fellow here to see you. Big fellow. Colored fellow. *Marshal* fellow."

I knew who that was. I took a final bite and stood. "Stay here and eat, Thalia. I'll be back directly." I headed outside.

Marshal Bass Reeves stood outside the tent, moonlight shining on him. A worn duster rested on his dark suit, his Marshal's badge pinned bold on his chest. He wasn't like one of them dress-up desperadoes from the Wild West Show. This man was a real gunslinger and we both knew it.

We shook hands. "Clarke."

“Marshal Reeves. You watch the show?”

“That I did.” He wasn’t smiling. “I’ve had worse times.” That was probably the best compliment I was gonna get out of him. “So, you’ve retired from bounty hunting, then. Taken up playing yourself in this show. Is that about the size of it?”

“It’s safer.” Attacking birds notwithstanding. “For me and Thalia.”

“Reckon that’s right. But I have need of your help, Clarke. Wouldn’t be here if I didn’t. And well, I thought you’d want to know.” He cleared his throat. “I’ll just come out and say it. Hell-Bound Hank Hoxton. He’s alive.”

Hell-Bound Hank Hoxton. It was like speaking of the war over dinner had conjured him up. Of all the bushwhackers and border ruffians I’d fought back then, Hoxton was the worst. He took to the revolver and Bowie knife like he’d been born to them, and he had men like William Quantrill and Bloody Bill Anderson as teachers. All those dead men and bodies in Lawrence. The butchered prisoners in Centralia. All the terror he’d sown, even after the war.

Until he vanished.

“How do you know?”

“Caught one of his compatriots who told me everything, in return for a reprieve from the hangman’s noose. Normally, I wouldn’t trust such a confession, but I’ve heard plenty of rumors over the years, and it makes sense. Hoxton is alive and he’s in Mexico. And according to this prisoner, he’s got some friends and they’re planning something.” He looked away, his hands in his pockets. “I can’t go to Mexico. Not legally. But you can. And you know him.”

I nodded. “Reckon so.”

“Think on it. I’ll be in town at the Grand.” He was already walking away.

Didn’t have to say more than that. I walked back into the tent, where laughter and questions greeted me. I hardly heard them. Nightmares of the war kept dancing in my head—my own father’s death amongst them. Hoxton hadn’t done that, but he’d done plenty more. And he’d never faced justice.

I was safe here. I was happy—more or less. More importantly, Thalia was safe.

But vengeance gnawed in my belly. I knew I was gonna go.

It was just a matter of time.

ABOUT OUR CREATORS

WRITER -

MICHAEL PANUSH is a lifelong writer. A born storyteller since childhood, Panush is the author of over a dozen books in numerous different genres. He's crafted Weird Westerns such as the El Mosaico and *Mark Justice's The Dead Sheriff: A Cold and Lonesome Grave* and the new Alternate History series, American Mammoths, Urban Fantasies like the Stein and Candle and Clay Shamus series, Woodland Medieval Fantasy with the *Tales of the Dark Forest*, and numerous stories that play with history in unique and wild ways such as the talking animal mystery Ape's Honor and The Stone Law, the tales of a Stone Age caveman detective.

With Charles Santino, he's created *Metropolis: Resurrection*—a prequel to the famous German Expressionist Sci-Fi Classic.

He lives and teaches in Sacramento.

Follow him on the web at https://michaelpanush.com/ and, on Instagram at @Michaelpanush and on Twitter at https://twitter.com/Michael_Panush

INTERIOR ILLUSTRATIONS -

RON HILL – has been an educational cartoonist, humorous illustrator, graphic designer, educator, author, armchair theologian and video documentarian (not all at the same time, of course!) for over 40 years. Born in Cleveland, he graduated from the Art Institute of Pittsburgh and immediately returned to Northeast Ohio to begin working in advertising.

In the 1980s-90s, as part of the illustration team of Lombardo & Hill, he drew countless interior illustrations for the role-playing games published by TSR, West End Games, Iron Crown Enterprises, and Chaosium, many involving licenses from the Lord of the Rings, Dungeons and Dragons, Indiana Jones and Star Wars. An accomplished quick-sketch caricature artist, he has drawn (to date) probably a quarter-million faces at thousands of private and public events from Chicago to New York. His editorial cartoons have appeared in the Chagrin Valley Times, Solon Times, Geauga Times Courier and West Life since 1999. In 2000 he started illustrating the popular "Armchair Theologian" book series for Westminster John-Knox; these 15 volumes have been translated into German, Japanese, Korean, Portuguese and Italian.

From 2002-2015, he taught in Interactive Media College Tech Prep program at Alliance High School, and has always conducted workshops at the area art centers (including the Valley Art Center) since 1990. After co-founding Act 3, a media company and indie publisher in Cleveland in 2016, he recently embarked (once again) on his solo career as a freelance artist, and is also currently working on a number of personal documentary projects, including "Go-Kart Therapy" and "We Are Doc Savage: A Documentary on Fandom. He has always lived in the Chagrin Valley of Northeast Ohio and you can learn more at www.RonHillArtist.com

He can be contacted and found here:
ArtistRonHill@gmail.com
RonHillArtist.com

COVER ARTIST -

ROB DAVIS - is an award-winning artist with a 38-plus-year comic book and illustration career. With comics from Marvel, DC, Malibu, Innovation, Caliber and others Rob has worked on series depicting the crews of *Star Trek*'s original series, *the Next Generation*, and *Deep Space Nine*, and other TV series such as *Quantum Leap* and *Pirates of Dark Water*. Characters like Merlin, Robin Hood, Zorro, and Sherlock Holmes have all been subjects of Rob's work. He is presently the Art Director, Designer, and Illustrator for Pulp Revival publisher Airship 27 Productions. He also self-publishes some of his most recent comic book work via his Redbud Studio imprint and is a contributor to Silverline Comics. He is retired from "real work" and lives in central Missouri with his wife, two children, and grandchildren.

www.ingramcontent.com/pod-product-compliance
Lightning Source LLC
LaVergne TN
LVHW010924110826
845149LV00013B/2476

* 9 7 8 1 9 6 9 2 8 5 0 8 0 *